Prince of
Nightmares

John McNee

BLOOD BOUND BOOKS

Copyright © 2016 by John McNee

All rights reserved

ISBN 978-1-940250-21-2

Artwork by Olga Noes

Interior Layout by Lori Michelle

Printed in the United States of America

First Edition

Visit us on the web at:
www.bloodboundbooks.net

ALSO FROM BLOOD BOUND BOOKS:

400 Days of Oppression by Wrath James White

Habeas Corpse by Nikki Hopeman

Mother's Boys by Daniel I. Russell

Fallow Ground by Michael James McFarland

Cradle of the Dead by Roger Jackson

Dark Waves by Simon Kearns

Loveless by Dev Jarrett

The Sinner by K. Trap Jones

The Return by David A. Riley

Knuckle Supper by Drew Stepek

Sons of the Pope by Daniel O'Connor

Dolls by KJ Moore

At the End of All Things by Stony Graves

The Black Land by MJ Wesolowski

Yeitso by Scott M. Baker

The River Through the Trees by David Peak

I lay me here to sleep;
No night-mare shall plague me,
Until they swim all the waters
That flow upon the earth,
And count all the stars
That appear in the firmament.
Thus help me God Father, Son, and Holy
  Ghost. Amen.

—Traditional German charm against
                              nightmares

Prologue

"**Sweet dreams**," her mother said, turning out the light.

Left alone to ponder the darkness, the girl didn't fret and didn't cry, but she didn't go to sleep. Though she was very young—too young to understand her mother's instructions—she seemed never to sleep.

She lay on her back in the crib, content to watch the shadows on the ceiling and wait patiently for something to happen.

For an hour or more she lay like that, though she was too young yet to appreciate the passage of time. Outside, the evening was a peaceful one, without even enough wind to shake the branches of the trees. Inside, the house was at rest, and silence reigned . . .

. . . until the music began.

Had she been able to lie another hour in the dark, listening only to the sound of her own breathing, she might well have slept. Eventually. The music dashed all hopes of that.

She lifted her head at the cheerful strumming of a guitar, stood as the rest of the band joined in and, at the sound of two pairs of feet dancing across the floorboards, pitched herself over the side of the crib.

She landed with a bump and was straight up onto her feet, toddling out through the door and down the hall, following the tune's echo to the bottom of the stairs, where a silver-plated, leather-lined wheelchair sat empty and abandoned.

Prince of Nightmares

On hands and knees she crawled up to the first floor landing, following the music to the library. A man was singing—his voice distorted by the vintage of the recording— though she was too young to understand the words.

Clinging to the door frame, keeping herself hidden, she peered in and saw a tall, old man dressed in tweed in the arms of a young, red-headed woman in a floral print dress. They grinned at each other, dancing across the open floor.

Behind them, seated in a wide circle, surrounded by mirrors, were ten or twelve others, among them her mother. They all laughed as the couple danced. They applauded.

She was too young to make sense of the scene. Too young to understand why they clapped their hands together, why the old man wept and cried out, "Thank you, Evelyn! Thank you so much!"

Looking past them, into the mirrors' reflections, she caught sight of a figure. None of the others seemed to see him—all too wrapped up in the dancing, laughing, weeping, and applause. She was the only one.

And he stared back.

A thin man of sharp, black shadow and smiling red eyes, he returned her gaze, regarding her with a warm familiarity that put her at ease instantly.

And though she was very young—too young to understand very much at all—she understood him.

The gunshot, when it came, was not quite loud enough to shock Victor out of his phone conversation. He jumped at the sound of the muffled pop from the bathroom, turning his head towards the locked door, but his concentration didn't waver.

"The steering group will need to see a report," he said. "Something substantial, before money changes hands."

"They want bribes is what they want," Edward's anxious voice echoed down the line from London, some 10,000 miles away. "Let's not be coy about this."

"Nonsense," said Victor, his gaze still on the bathroom door, eyes narrowed, wondering what it was he'd just heard. "They just need a few pages of crap to wade through. A few graphs." Surely Josie had heard it too. "Edward, can I call you back?"

"They want to see something now," Edward answered. "This week. And I'm in no position . . . I'm flying to Munich on Tuesday."

Victor raised himself slowly from the bed, eyes on the door, searching the wall for answers, wondering what could have made a sound like that. "Edward, call Crawford. He'll be at the conference. He can help you. Slater will have his number."

"Carlford?"

"No. *Crawford*," Victor snarled, fingers tightening around the receiver, eager to be free. "C-R-A-W-F-O-R-D. Ask Slater. I have to go now."

Prince of Nightmares

"All right, then. Thank you, Mr Tev—"

He slammed the receiver down and crossed towards the bathroom door.

It was all over, and had been since the shot had sounded. There was nothing he could have done in those few moments, no way to help. But, in the months to come, the memory of those seconds frittered away on meaningless conversation would haunt him.

The bathroom door wasn't locked. It clicked open at his touch. Josie's name was on his lips, but he never got it out. The smell stifled any words—the fierce odour of burnt cordite and something more. He leaned around the door, his mind's eye already two jumps ahead, telling him what he would discover. There would be no surprises here.

Blood was spattered on the inside of the shower curtain.

When he cast his mind back to the discovery, he wouldn't remember crossing from the door to the bathtub, but he must have run, because in a flash he was there, hand gripping the curtain and tearing it back, revealing her as she'd wanted him to see her, as she'd wanted him to *remember* her—a glorious, gore-slicked disgrace, a hideous jumble of pale, bony limbs and blood, sickening in its lack of dignity, to be forever seared upon his memory. The brand of a vicious and spiteful lover.

She still clung to the revolver with both hands, the edge of the gun barrel lodged between her teeth. Smoke spiralled upward from the jagged cavity at the back of her skull.

Victor could hear the shot now, he realized. Over and over again it thundered in his head. And a voice. Her voice? His own?

No. *Don't be stupid*, he told himself. The phantom gunshots were fists pounding on the hotel room door. The voice was Harry's.

A moment later someone from hotel security slid their card into the lock and they all came piling in to find what he had found, and the man himself, old and broken. He was crouched at the side of the tub—looking like he might never find the strength to lift himself back to his feet—and was reaching out with one liver-spotted hand towards his dead wife, unable to bring himself to touch her.

"Oh no . . . " said Harry, finding the words that Victor could not.

He turned slowly, expecting to meet the man's gaze, but saw Harry was not looking at him, nor at Josie's corpse. His eyes were on the mirror, drawing Victor's attention to the last horror in the room—the suicide note he'd failed to see.

It was scrawled in her lipstick: *God forgive me. I married an evil man.*

A tap on the window roused him from a dreamless sleep.

"Victor! Wake up, we're here."

He blinked the smudges from his sight and cringed, cursing himself for drifting off. Dozing in the back of cars—even Bentleys—was bad for his joints. He could feel the familiar stiffness creeping its way into his knees and neck muscles even as he tossed *Private Eye* out of his lap and reached for his walking cane.

"You shouldn't have let me sleep," he growled as he stepped out.

"I was driving," said Harry.

There had been no need in Harry coming along all the way from Sydney, babysitting him on two flights and acting as chauffeur the last 100 miles. Victor had told him so, but Harry insisted.

He found his footing on the gravel and squinted up the sloping hill to the Ballador House Hotel. It was a handsome Gothic building, characterized by turrets, bay windows, and stained glass, but undeniably modest.

"That's not a castle, is it?" asked Harry. "I was expecting a castle."

"It is what it is," Victor muttered, turning away. He looked across the car park to the loch, silver and still in the early evening breeze.

"I'll take the bags in," Harry said.

"Do that," Victor said, starting downhill toward the water. "I'll join you in a minute."

John McNee

The sun was white and small in the west, but still just visible under a veil of grey cloud. Victor clutched at the collar of his overcoat and took a lungful of cool air, hoping it and the silence might flush some of the clutter from his head.

There were no boats on the water, no people on the pebble shore. The hills on the other side of the loch were pale purple shadows, showing no signs of life. It felt like he was a very long way from civilization.

He entered the lobby to find Harry arguing with the woman at the desk.

"Well, it's not acceptable," he was saying, sounding like the definitive loud-mouth Yank abroad. "You're supposed to be running a professional business. Someone reserves a room, you hold it for them. You don't just give it away when you feel like it. I wouldn't think I'd have to explain that to a hotel manager."

"Well no, of course, and I do apologize. I never imagined there would be a problem." The woman had a helmet of orange hair that looked tough enough to smash glass. On her tartan jacket was a gold name tag that read: SHONA DEMPSEY—MANAGER.

"What's going on?" Victor asked.

"She's given your room away," Harry said. His face was flushed, which happened with alarming speed whenever he got upset about something. Even his eyes, behind the thick tortoise-shell glasses, looked red.

"Not *given away* exactly," the manager protested. "We have two suites. Circumstances required that I swap reservations so that another guest moved into your suite and you took theirs."

"So?" Victor said.

Harry stamped his finger on the counter. "Mrs Teversham—the *late* Mrs Teversham—specifically reserved the Library Suite."

"The amenities are the same," she said. "There's no difference in price."

"I don't understand," Victor interjected. "What suite would I be getting?"

Harry shot a challenging glare to the manager. She hesitated, looking back and forth between the pair before admitting, "The . . . Honeymoon Suite."

"Ah," Victor said. Suddenly it all made sense.

"Do you have any idea who this man is?" Harry snapped, building to another rant. Decades spent travelling the globe in the employ of Victor Teversham had dulled the edges of his Boston accent, but it reaffirmed itself with vigour when he got mad. "You'd physically have to have your head stuck up your ass not to have the faintest inkling of what he's had to endure these . . . "

"Harry," Victor said. "Forget it. It's fine."

"It's *not* fine," Harry barked, then hushed when he realized how much noise he was making. The argument had turned the heads of more than one customer in the bar area. "Victor, it's not fine," he whispered. "It's the Honeymoon Suite."

"It's just a room, Harry," Victor said, wanting an end to the conversation. "Four walls and a bed. It doesn't matter."

"Victor—"

"It doesn't matter." He approached the desk. "Is there something I need to sign?"

The manager nodded stiffly and put some papers before him. "I'll need the card that was used to make the reservation."

"My wife's card," Victor said, opening his wallet. "Here's mine."

"You're . . . aware of what a stay here entails, aren't you? You know of our reputation?" she asked as she handed his card back to him.

Harry snorted derisively.

"Yes," Victor said. "I've been told all about it."

"Okay," she said and reached for another piece of paper. "Then I also have to ask you to sign this. It just protects us against litigation in the event of any psychological or physical trauma."

"Don't sign that," Harry said. "Don't sign a damn thing." Again he turned on the manager. "Nothing on your website said anything about signing any waivers. What kind of bullshit scam are you trying to run?"

"I . . . " the woman stammered. "I just . . . it's . . . "

Victor scratched his name across the page. "Just give me the key."

Mrs Dempsey took the waiver and smiled curtly, but neglected to make eye contact with either man as she filed it and went through to the office.

"Victor . . . " Harry pressed in towards him, speaking in conspiratorial tones. "Are you absolutely sure about this?"

Victor sighed. "How many more times do you think you're going to ask me that?"

Mrs Dempsey returned with the key and waved them towards the stairs. "Right this way, gentlemen."

The two suites took up the whole of the country house's first floor. The Library Suite comprised the rooms at the rear of the house, facing the trees, while Victor's quarters looked out across the loch. A brass plate on the door confirmed it as the "Honeymoon Suite" in delicately engraved script, but inside there were thankfully few reminders of its romantic status.

The suite included a large sitting room with a carved fireplace and turreted dining area, adjoining a king-sized bedroom and en-suite bathroom. It was warmly furnished throughout in antique oak and tweed, and Victor felt willing to concede that under different circumstances he'd probably have found it all quite charming.

Harry gazed out at the loch. "Not exactly Miami Beach, but I guess it's okay."

Victor shook off his overcoat and hung it up. "It'll do."

"Honeymoon Suite," Harry sneered. "What's a place like

this need a honeymoon suite for, anyway? Who seriously wants to spend their honeymoon in a haunted house?"

Victor sniffed and shrugged. "There are some strange people in the world, I suppose."

"You're right about that. I think I saw a few in the lobby." Harry turned away from the window and surveyed the room. "You want me to help you unpack?"

"I'm not a bloody child, Harry."

"I didn't say you were," he protested.

"I can unpack my own bloody suitcases, okay? You've done more than enough. More than I ever needed or expected you to."

"Clearly."

Victor sighed. "I'm not having a go, all right?"

"You're upset about the woman at the desk, aren't you? I can go talk to her, if you want, and smooth things over."

"No, no," Victor said. "I can do that. You need to get a move on. It'll be dark soon."

"Right." Harry hesitated. "Of course . . . I could always ask if there are any rooms free . . . without ghosts?"

"No."

"Or there was a motel we passed, just before the bridge. I would be just up the road."

"No, no. Don't degrade yourself on my account, please."

"I don't like leaving you here on your own."

"I want to be on my own!" He was shouting now. "Don't you get it? I *need* to be on my own!"

"It's not right, Victor. It's not healthy."

"Jesus Christ, not again," he moaned. "Not this again."

"Again? I've been biting my damn tongue since Stansted!"

"I'm not going to kill myself," he yelled. "I'm not waiting for you to leave so I can tie a rope around my neck! I'm not going to slash my throat with a razor and I'm not about to swallow a bunch of pills and go walking into the lake! I just need to be alone."

"There are better places for grieving."

Victor gave a bitter laugh as he collapsed into one of the armchairs, as though the argument was physically exhausting him. "Don't talk to me about grief. She wanted it this way. For better or worse. She chose this. That makes it the best chance I have at understanding."

Harry shook his head. "You won't find any answers here, Victor."

He closed his eyes and felt the pain behind them. "Maybe not. But at least it'll get me away from you for a little while, eh?" He smiled. "Come on, you must need a vacation as badly as me. When's the last time you had four whole days away from my ugly face?"

Harry did his best to return the smile, but it still came off a little half-hearted. "I honestly can't remember." He was quieter now, like a dog that had been brought to heel.

Victor clapped his hand on the armrest of his chair. "There you are, you see? Likely do us both a bit of good."

"It's been so long. I don't know what to do with myself."

"Treat it as a learning experience. We both can."

"Yeah, I guess." Harry nodded, satisfied there was nothing more he could say. "You got your cell phone?"

Victor chuckled. "No, Harry, I don't have my cell phone."

"Oh Victor, come on!"

"No. There was a time before bloody cell phones, Wi-Fi, satellite television and all the other feckless distractions of the world. You may not remember it, but I do, and I bloody well *long* for it. That's what I want. So no, I don't have my cell, but you know where I am if you need to reach me and I have your number if I absolutely have to call you." He gave the other man a hard glare. "I *won't* call you. Please try not to call here."

Harry nodded. "Well. See you in four days, I guess."

"All right." Victor didn't rise from his chair. Instead, he turned his head towards the window, staring out at the ashen sky. "See you then."

Harry walked out of the suite and closed the door behind

him. He strolled down the stairs and straight out through the main doors, pausing only briefly in the lobby near a rack of brochures and guidebooks. He pocketed one on his way out— a narrow digest with a glossy maroon cover and raised black title that read: History of Ballador House.

He was alone.

He remained in the chair for close to an hour watching the sky, like a sheet of stretched grey plastic, gradually darkening as the sun sank behind the hills. He heard the pop of gravel in the drive as Harry departed. And he could hear the faint sounds of other guests in other rooms, or making their way up or down the stairs. Eventually though, all he could hear was the sound of his own breath and the soft thump of his own heart in his chest.

He was alone.

It was, he realised, the first time he'd been alone, properly, since Josie's death. The last time might even have been years or decades before that. Wherever he'd gone or whatever he'd done, she had been there. And if not her, then Harry or any dozen of his other flunkies. No matter what he was doing there was always another meeting to get to, another phone call to take, another mess to clean up, another policeman to pay off, politician to flatter, or journalist to intellectually eviscerate. Never a moment to himself.

In the weeks following Josie's death, the calls, texts, and emails had thinned out, but there always seemed to be people in the room. At home, the only time Harry or the housekeeping staff let him be was when he was sleeping or defecating.

This was different. Quite different.

Victor rose from the chair and went into the bedroom. A dressing table with a large mirror stood against one wall. He crept towards it, regarding his haggard reflection like a wild, wounded animal.

He made for a sorry sight. His body was thin yet sagging and already bearing the hunch of a drying spine. His skin had the pallor of cheap putty—a consequence of living too long in England—and looked much like it had been stretched across his skull by a crazed toddler, pulled too tight across his forehead and cheeks, but hanging in wrinkled bunches under his chin. Dry white hair sprouted proudly around his ears and the back of his neck, but nowhere else on his head, while his watery blue eyes peered grimly out of dark, sunken sockets.

He'd clothed his aching limbs in a pressed white shirt and charcoal suit, rumpled and musty from travelling, and finished with a plain black tie.

Regarding himself now, he saw a frail old man, dressed as though for his own funeral.

"Stop it," he said, shaking the morbid thought from his head.

He undid the tie as he reached for the nearest suitcase. He changed, putting on a pair of corduroy trousers, green knitted jumper and brown brogues. Not the most remarkable of transformations perhaps, but he felt better about his reflection when he checked the mirror again.

He thought of splashing some water over his face, but hesitated on his way to the en suite and doubled back into the sitting room. He picked up his cane on the way out the door and headed down to the lobby.

The manager was still behind the desk when he arrived at the bottom of the stairs. She was reading something from a stack of forms and looked to be typing it into the computer. If Victor had wanted to, he could have probably walked right by without her noticing, but that would only have prolonged the inevitable.

"Pardon me," he said, as timidly as he could. "I just want to apologise for my friend's behaviour earlier. It was . . . uncalled for."

Mrs Dempsey raised her head and, for the briefest

moment, flashed a look that was hard rage. It softened in the next instant, to be replaced by gentle affability. "It's really quite all right, Mr Teversham. The fault was mine."

"Whether there was any fault or not is irrelevant. His tone and comments were entirely unacceptable."

She smiled. "Oh, I've had to deal with a lot worse, believe me. You quickly get used to it doing this job."

"Unruly guests?"

"A few. Our reputation attracts the occasional odd sort. Quite a few odd sorts, if I'm honest. You'll probably meet some of them. They can be keen to swap stories of the things they've seen. And equally keen to apportion blame when they see something they don't like."

"Oh, come now," he said. "Can it really be that bad?"

She shrugged with her eyebrows—the kind of expression that said, *You don't know what you're letting yourself in for and I've no way of communicating it.* "Put it this way," she said. "I've slept here only once. That was ten years ago. And it'll be another hundred before I do it again."

He didn't have a reply to that. He stared at her for a few seconds with his mouth slightly open, trying to gauge if she was joking. Finally, still undecided, he said, "I was going to enquire about getting something to eat."

"Ah, yes!" The woman's tone and expression brightened remarkably. "Our restaurant is straight through the lounge or, if you'd prefer privacy, an order can be made straight to your suite."

"The restaurant sounds preferable."

"Very good." She logged out of the hotel computer and rounded the desk. "I'll take you through."

She led him into the lounge—decorated in more oak panelling and mercifully muted shades of tartan—and past the bar, through French doors into the dining room.

"Dinner is served from five until ten," she said. "But the bar is open twenty-four hours with a limited menu if you should find yourself peckish in the night."

"I wouldn't have thought there were enough guests to merit that," Victor said.

"We may not have a great number, but the ones we do have can be prone to restless nights. We like to provide a comfortable area where they can come, relax, have a drink, and share stories, whatever the hour. Personally, I think it's worth it. Many have said so. But you'll find all that out for yourself, I'm sure." She gave him another smile laced with friendly malevolence and motioned to a waiter. "Mr Teversham of the Honeymoon Suite," she said, when the young man approached. "For dinner."

The waiter—a tall, thin lad, not quite out of his teens, with bleach-blond hair and an earring through his eyebrow— nodded and escorted Victor to a table by the window, thankfully making no enquiries as to whether his wife would be joining him.

"Can I get you something to drink?"

"Ginger ale for now," Victor said. "No ice."

The pierced waiter left him to peruse the menu and wine list. Victor surveyed the room. Of the ten or so tables, only three were occupied, including his. At the one farthest away sat a middle-aged couple, quietly sipping soup without looking each other in the eye. On Victor's right, against the opposite wall, another man was dining alone. He looked only ten or fifteen years younger than Victor, dressed in a chequered suit and bow tie. Victor couldn't identify what the man was eating. Some kind of obscure meat dish.

He scanned his own menu. Breast of Scottish wood pigeon, rouge foie gras, veal sweetbreads. There was no shortage of contenders. When he glanced up, he saw that the man was staring at him. He had wide, pale eyes, accentuated by the deep tan of his skin.

Victor immediately looked away, turning his attention back to the menu. He could tell, however, that the other guest had not turned away. The eyes were still on him. He could feel them.

"Ginger ale," the waiter said, announcing his return and setting the glass down. "Are you ready to order?"

"Yes, I think so." Victor ordered a Roquefort salad followed by venison wellington. The only pinot noir on the wine list was from New Zealand, but he grit his teeth and ordered a bottle anyway.

The waiter nodded, gathered the menus and started back to the kitchen. When he stepped away, the man at the other table returned to his peripheral vision. Victor was well-used to being stared at. People didn't fawn over him the way they might a film star or pop singer, but he had, in his life, managed to achieve a certain level of notoriety. This had spiked in recent weeks, with Josephine's death—and its investigation—making international headlines. He was well-practised in the art of ignoring rubberneckers. He'd come prepared for it. Yet, there was something about this character that unsettled him.

He turned his head towards the window. He gazed at the newer part of the hotel, which was built in the nineties. As he understood it, those six rooms weren't afflicted with the same phenomenon that supposedly blighted his, meaning the Ballador was at least halfway able to operate as a mainstream tourist destination. The architects had taken great care imitating the style of the original design and the materials looked very close, but a shrewd eye could easily tell where the old joined the new. Beyond this was a well-maintained lawn with a few shrubs and flower beds, then woodlands, and beyond that more hills, their crests just visible against the darkening sky. He turned back just as the first drops of rain began to patter against the glass.

The tanned man's eyes were still on him. It suddenly occurred to Victor that the man was wearing mascara, the same boot polish shade as the hair he'd combed taught over his scalp and shaved into a pencil-thin moustache above his lips. Those lips . . .

Victor glanced down to his ginger ale, focussing on its

carbonated bubbles. He raised it to his mouth, closing his eyes as he took a long sip. He kept them closed as he lowered the glass to the table, clenched and unclenched his fists, sucked a deep breath in through his mouth, let it out through his nostrils. Those lips . . .

Finally, his eyes snapped open and he turned them on the other diner, delivering a good hard glare. The gentleman gave no sign of embarrassment or even acknowledgement. He held Victor's gaze. Victor squinted, focusing his attention on the man's mouth and confirming his suspicions.

He was wearing lipstick—pink, with a wet gloss finish. As Victor stared, the ends of his pink lips curled upwards into an incomprehensible smile.

Victor responded the only way he knew how. He rose from his chair, stormed across the room towards the other man's table, then continued straight out through the door.

"On reflection, I think I'm a little more tired than I first realised," he told Mrs Dempsey when he reached the front desk. "I'll take dinner in my suite."

"Certainly, sir. I'll inform the kitchen."

He trudged wearily back up the stairs, trying to shake the image of the pink-lipped man out of his head. He had anticipated there would be strange characters here. What he hadn't expected was just how uncomfortable he could be made to feel in their presence. He'd thought himself much tougher to rattle.

Arriving on the first floor, he tried his key in the lock and found it wouldn't fit. He sighed, tried it again, tugged at the handle, slammed his palm against the door and failed to move it a millimetre. It was only when he took a step back that he realised he was standing outside the wrong suite. He heard someone moving inside, and before he could flee, the door was thrown open.

The brunette who emerged was young, beautiful, and visibly outraged. Victor saw her bare feet first and even they looked angry. Raising his head he quickly took in her long legs, short satin nightgown and fair, freckled face, framed by a tousled mess of brown hair. Her features were screwed up in fury, a French curse word on the tip of her tongue. Yet when her eyes met Victor's they popped wide. Her jaw dropped and she jerked back, slamming the door in his face before he could muster anything approaching an apology.

"S-sorry . . . " he said, directing his apology to the brass plate that read: The Library Suite.

Though embarrassment had slightly dented his appetite, he made it to the end of his meal, enjoyed in relative tranquillity. A large flat screen television was concealed in a cabinet in the living room, but he consciously ignored it. It was tempting to seek distractions from his own thoughts, but that would contradict his entire purpose in coming to the hotel. So he ate accompanied by the sound of the rain, which lasted only until the end of his second course.

When he was done, he put the tray on the sideboard outside his door—casting a nervous glance at the door to the other suite across the landing—and prepared for bed.

Again, he slowed as he neared the en suite, trying to block unpleasant thoughts and images from creeping into his mind but not quite succeeding. The journey brought the memories rushing back. His footsteps were so much like the steps he'd taken that night. Standing at the bathroom's door felt like standing at an aeroplane's hatch, steeling himself to take a leap into the void.

With heavy breaths he pushed the door open and turned on the light. The en suite was tiled in white and blue with old-fashioned porcelain fittings. The bathtub was on his right, half-hidden by an opaque plastic shower curtain. Of course it was.

He felt dizzy and weak as he reached his hand out towards it, gripped and peeled it back to reveal what he already knew he'd find.

Prince of Nightmares

Nothing.
It didn't matter. He saw her there anyway.

Gia sat on the arm of the couch, bare feet tapping anxiously on the rug. Her thumb was between her teeth, eyes fixed on a distant point beyond the room, trying to unravel an impossible problem. She didn't hear the knocking at first, but when she did, she stiffened, immediately alarmed by the thought of who or what might be standing outside.

"Who's there?" she yelled.

"It's Heinrich!" His voice had a jovial sing-song quality to it that instantly set her teeth on edge.

"Leave me alone!" No sooner were the words out of her mouth than she was on her feet, storming across the room to the door and throwing it wide. "What do you want?"

He smiled his pink lips at her and ran his eyes up and down her body. "I brought wine." He raised a bottle in one hand and a pair of glasses in the other.

She scowled. "That's the best you can do?"

He raised a dyed eyebrow. "It's . . . not bad wine."

"Leave me alone, Heinrich. I'm not in the mood."

He cocked his head to one side, giving her another appraisal, trying to discern the cause of her current mood. "You've seen him, haven't you?"

Her scowl deepened. "Get in."

The smile on his face shifted suddenly into a smirk as he crossed the threshold and made for the small dining table, where a tuna sandwich sat, going stale. He brushed it out of his way, set down the glasses and began to pour the wine.

Gia closed the door and put her back up against it. "Who is he?"

Prince of Nightmares

"You don't know?"

She bit her lip by way of reply.

Heinrich shrugged and filled the second glass. "Victor Teversham. Multi-millionaire industrial tycoon."

"Tycoon?"

"Hmmm? Oh, you know . . . um . . . magnate. Very rich and very powerful."

"But what does that mean? What does he do?"

Heinrich took the glasses to the couch and sat down. "I don't know that he does anything. He's very rich and very powerful. People do things for him. Whatever he wants them to do."

Gia rolled her eyes. "You're a fountain of information, Heinrich."

"At least I've heard of him. You ought to pick up a newspaper once in a while."

She frowned. "We're definitely talking about the same person, right?"

"The little old man living in the suite across from you?"

"Yes."

"Then yes. Are you going to share a drink with me or not?"

She stood her ground at the door for another moment, then padded across the carpet to the couch, but didn't sit down beside him. She took the glass from his hand and moved to the window. "What's he doing here?" she asked.

"That's the question, isn't it?"

"One of them." She looked down into the garden, where only the smokers tended to tread after dark. There was one of them down there now—a woman in a grey overcoat, standing just beyond a row of acutely-trimmed hedges. She had her back to the hotel, gazing off into the trees. "I'd like to know what he's doing here."

"You could always ask him, I suppose. I'm sure he wouldn't mind being approached by a fragrant young thing like you."

"He might. He came to my door earlier. By mistake, I suppose. When I saw it was him, I was so shocked I slammed the door in his face."

"Mmmm. I didn't fair much better, I'm afraid."

Gia turned to look at him. "You spoke to him?"

Heinrich shrugged. "Not quite. There was . . . an *encounter* in the dining room. He left quite abruptly."

"You mean you freaked him out."

"It wasn't my intent."

"No, you just have a natural talent for that, don't you? Making people uncomfortable."

He pursed his lips and furrowed his brow in a mock expression of concern. "Do I make you uncomfortable, my dear?"

She smiled. "No, Heinrich. You don't. But I think that says rather more about me than it does about you." She sipped her wine and turned back to the window. The woman at the hedgerow hadn't moved.

"You're dressed for the bedroom," Heinrich said. Though she wasn't facing him, Gia could feel his eyes on her again, lingering on her legs. "Have you ventured past the door at all today?"

"What would be the point of that? I have almost everything I need here. Room service brings me the rest."

He looked again at the sad sandwich on the table. "But you don't eat."

"I've no appetite."

"No. Not for food. You hunger for other delights."

She cringed. "I wish you wouldn't try to be poetic. I find it difficult enough to follow the threads of our conversations. Start getting all romantic with me and you might as well be talking German."

"You shouldn't spend so much time in here," he insisted. "You can't sleep the whole day away."

"I can try."

"You can't. No one can try to sleep. The body wants to rest

or it doesn't. You need to first put yourself through some kind of physical exertion. Wear out the flesh."

She scoffed. "If that's why you came here then you're definitely out of luck. I don't intend to go wearing out my flesh with you." She raised her glass. "I'm sure this'll do just fine. No offence."

He shifted irritably. "You're so very quick to assume I always mean only one thing. I'm serious. I'm trying to help you. Tomorrow you must get out of the hotel. Go do something. Head into town, go for a walk, take a boat on the water. Do something to exhaust yourself. I'm sure the skin-ripping hooks and ballet dancing will be waiting for you when you return."

Gia shook her head. "That's the wrong dream. The one I had before I came here."

"Ah." Heinrich took a long sip of wine. "Forgive me. But, now I think of it, I don't believe you've described to me any of the ones you've had since you've been here."

Gia didn't reply. She was watching the woman in the garden, who still hadn't turned around. Gia was suddenly seized by the realisation that she didn't *want* her to turn around. Rather, she wanted anything other than to see the woman's face. It was a notion that frightened her both in its content and the manner by which it so immediately permeated her thoughts, enveloping her consciousness like poison vapour. And so, what a moment before had seemed pedestrian now held her in the grip of fear. Scared to speak, scared to move, scared to close her eyes, but, above all else, scared that the woman might suddenly look round towards the hotel and reveal herself.

The fear held her in place, kept her staring dead ahead as the woman shifted ever so slowly, turning to her left and walking away, following the hedgerows as they tapered towards the window frame, beyond Gia's field of vision. The woman moved with the languid pace of a pallbearer and Gia could feel her pulse accelerating beyond each tortuous step

John McNee

as she kept her eyes on the back of her head. *Don't look at me,* she thought. *Please. Please don't look at me.*

With one step to go, Gia caught the slight tilt of the woman's head and a flick of her short, dark hair that very nearly caused her heart to seize. And then she was gone. Out of sight, and very nearly, out of mind.

"Gia?"

"Hmmm?"

"Are you all right?"

She nodded. "Yes. Yes, I'm fine." The fear had receded as quickly as it had come, melting into no more than a half-felt memory. It didn't feel like her own. It felt comical. She lifted the glass to her lips and smiled, feeling almost proud of the way she could still so effectively frighten herself with a delicate thought. "Did you ask me something?"

"In a way," said Heinrich. "I just wondered if you were ready to share with me any of the things you've seen." He waved towards her bedroom. "In that charming little room over there."

She considered for a moment. "No. Not quite yet."

I͟t͟ ͟s͟t͟a͟r͟t͟e͟d͟ ͟w͟i͟t͟h͟ a sound like rustling paper.

Victor was still awake. It wasn't fear or lack of nerve that kept him conscious. It was more a dull, uninvited anticipation. He knew he couldn't be the first guest to experience this. He surprised himself for not having thought of it before. How was a man supposed to relax enough to fall asleep when he'd been promised nightmares?

He lay in bed, sheets drawn over his chest, gazing up through the four-poster's vacant canopy to the ceiling. He stared at the cornicing, just visible in the shadows, running in intricate semi-circles around the edges of the room. He had been staring at the cornicing for more than two hours now and wondered how many more hours would be lost to its study in the evenings to come.

This is how they do it, of course, he thought. *This is their whole business model, right here.* It was depressingly simple when you stopped to think about it. Ballador House had built a reputation for nightmares, flying in the face of logic and all basic scientific understanding. Harry himself had argued the point with Victor.

"Dreams are of the mind," he'd told him, back when the subject had first surfaced. "Locked in the subconscious. They don't creep their way into your head like little monsters. They're a part of you. The ground you're sleeping on, the bed, the building around it . . . they shouldn't matter. You simply can't guarantee nightmares. It's not possible."

He argued the point emphatically, despite reading the

verified accounts of previous guests who described experiences "beyond anything the conscious mind could conceive," "vivid as life," and "better than any horror film ever made or that ever could be made."

Both he and Victor had been so dogmatic in their discussions that they had failed to see the obvious. In order to guarantee nightmares all the hotel really had to do was guarantee nightmares. The subconscious did the rest.

Victor himself was evidence of that. Still wide awake in spite of crushing exhaustion, all because someone had promised him something extraordinary when he closed his eyes. It wasn't that he was a true believer. It was the *possibility* that kept his mind churning into the night. Like a child anxiously awaiting Christmas morning, only worse, because in that case sleep was simply a barrier. It wasn't the focus of every kind of unease.

Send a man to bed promising horror and he'll lie awake thinking about it. And when at last the veil of slumber falls it will be a fitful, feverish sleep, beset by the same lingering dreads. Such was the power of suggestion.

The realization didn't bring him any comfort, nor clear his mind of furious thought. He closed his eyes and rolled onto his side. And that's when he heard it.

A whisper of movement, like air on cotton. Barely a sound at all. Victor heard it, but almost dismissed it. Buildings as old as this one made noises all the time.

The next sound was like that.

Crumbling plaster in the walls, pieces of grit scratching against each other. Or vermin. He supposed it wasn't beyond the realms of possibility for a few mice to have sneaked into the skirting boards. Slowly, he raised his head from the pillow, turning in the direction of the sound. It was coming from the corner of the room, he realised. Not a corner of the floor, but the ceiling. A jittery confusion of fibres, sandpaper or dry leaves.

No. None of those.

Prince of Nightmares

He blinked, irritation rising, as the noise persisted, quieter than the tick of a clock but too loud to ignore. It sounded like a tissue man feverishly rubbing his hands together. Victor frowned, the image lingering in his mind, and said to himself, "That's a strange thing to think."

He pulled back the covers and eased his legs over the side of the bed, ignoring the way his tired limbs cried out at being put to work again so soon. After two half-hearted, unsuccessful attempts, he forced himself up onto his feet, arching his back and stretching his neck, hearing them pop angrily. Rubbing his eyes and yawning, he stumbled around the end of the bed, making his way to the bathroom, and then stopped.

A woman stood in the middle of the floor, her back turned to him. Crooked arms and a narrow body filled a long, ragged dress, all the colour of deep, dark shadow. She moved without sound, swaying with her arms over her head, like seaweed in water.

Victor couldn't understand what he was seeing. His own body was frozen, breath trapped in his chest as he watched her, gently writhing in rhythm to a silent song.

The scene continued that way for a while. He didn't know if she was aware of him in the room or not. She danced as though lost in a dream of her own.

When, finally, she turned toward him, shuffling in jerky but unhurried movements, he saw her face was hidden by an undulating black veil. Her dress seemed almost organic, quivering out of time with her own movements and sprouting wiry fingers that curled and snapped at the air.

Her warped arms twisted and bent like rubber in wave-like motions that he soon realized were intended to coax him towards her. Triple-jointed fingers spread from her knuckles like a thousand untidy branches from a sapling. Each coiled and uncoiled its own invitation.

As grotesque as the woman appeared, Victor could feel himself yielding to her, longing for her phantom embrace. With a sudden burst of urgency, he crossed the floor to meet her, letting the forest of her arms close about him.

She enveloped him in darkness and let a welcoming groan rise out of her throat. But not her lips. As the veil peeled back, Victor saw she had no face.

Beneath the fringe of her slick hair was only a yawning chasm, as though half of her head had been scooped clean, exposing a crater of putrid black flesh. Her abundance of fingers wrapped themselves worm-like about his body, tight to the skin, ice-cold and brittle. They looped around his wrists and ankles, gripped his hips and stuck fast to his neck and head.

I'm dreaming, he thought.

She began to laugh. It erupted out of the black void of her head and bounced off the walls, growing louder with echo. "Kiss me," she said, speaking without a mouth, pulling him closer. "Then tell me you're dreaming."

She snapped his head forward, forcing his mouth into the wet pulverised matter where her face should have been. He resisted, overcome with revulsion. With his lips pressed against her cold flesh he felt something pulsating beneath—something warm forcing its way up through her soft tissue. Her tongue came to meet his. He fought without chance of success. His jaw opened almost of its own accord and her moist muscle pressed between his teeth to wrap around his own tongue, before stretching to the back of his throat and sliding down his oesophagus.

The intrusion caused him to spasm in shock.

A moment more and her fingers followed her tongue's example, seeking out every orifice on his body and invading. He wanted to scream, but her fat tongue choked him. Thin fingers slid up his nostrils, into his ears. They invaded his pyjamas and slithered their way into his anus and urethra. When all his holes were filled, new holes were made. Razor-tipped fingers pierced his wrists, stomach, back, and shoulders. Needle-thin digits burrowed into his scalp and forced their way into the space between his eyeball and socket. The pain was unimaginable. Unendurable. His flesh burned.

Prince of Nightmares

Thousands of her cold fingers stretched and snaked within him, treating his veins like footpaths, his intestines like highways, forcing deeper and deeper, knifing into his flesh, deeper into his organs, deeper and deeper and deeper, coiling about his brain. Her voice called to him in his mind, echoing within his skull. *"Hush now. We haven't . . . even . . . begun."*

Finally, her grasping digits sought out what she was after and, with a crushing hand, she laid claim to his soul.

Opening his eyes felt like prying open a closed wound. Reality was another layer of torture, but he fought with more energy than he knew he had to force his eyelids apart.

He lay on the bed, sprawled out on his back in the dark, staring up at the ceiling. The cornicing grinned down at him.

He felt pinned to the mattress, unable to move a single finger, like the blood had been squeezed out of his veins and replaced with cement. Sweat beaded his face and dampened the sheets under his back. His breaths came in pained, choking gasps through a throat that felt raw, while his heart pounded urgently in his chest, straining under an invisible weight.

He was awake. He *knew* he was awake, but he couldn't move. Why couldn't he move?

And he wasn't alone. He was certain of that. A creature twitched, unseen, on top of him, close enough that he could feel the ripples in the air when it came near his face, close enough that he could hear the dry, fidgeting cacophony it made. Like rustling paper.

Victor's moment of clarity didn't last for long. Less than five seconds later fresh weights found his eyelids and drew them down, plunging him back into the darkest depths of the dream, snuffing out his last most coherent thought.

There's something in the room with me. Something with wings.

He ordered porridge for breakfast and, when it arrived, wondered why. None of his actions over the course of the morning had any real thought behind them. He'd managed to wash, dress, and make it down to the dining room without ever really waking up. When the waiter approached, Victor was somehow able to ape the behaviour of a typical human being, but now the fog was beginning to clear and he was staring into the porridge bowl, spoon in hand, with no desire to eat.

"Excuse me? Hello? Pardon me." Victor turned to find he was being addressed by the man at the table next to him—a scrawny, bearded Englishman halfway through a cooked breakfast. His plump young girlfriend sat opposite, hand over her eyes, clearly overcome with embarrassment. "I'm sorry to disturb you," he said. "But I have to ask . . . did you see her?"

"I, um . . . what?" Victor said.

"You're in the Honeymoon Suite, aren't you?" The man wore a greasy ponytail to complement his beard, along with a pair of glasses that Victor guessed would have been painfully unfashionable thirty years ago.

"I am," he replied, indulging the man against better judgement. There was something vaguely idiotic about the way he grinned, the way he spoke, but Victor tried not to let his immediate contempt show through.

"Then you must have seen her, right?" the man asked. "The Drowned Maid?"

Prince of Nightmares

The girl moaned. "Paul . . . "

"I honestly don't know what you're talking about," Victor said.

Paul laughed excitedly, delighted to discover Victor hadn't done his homework. "The Honeymoon Suite was originally the master bedroom," he said. "Back in 1868, the house was owned by Logan Thomas, who lived here with his wife while carrying on an affair with his housemaid. The story goes that she got pregnant and threatened to expose him, so he killed her and dumped her body in the loch. But at night she would return to him in his sleep, tormenting him in his dreams. The visions drove him past the point of madness, until eventually he rowed back out onto the loch one night . . . and was never seen again."

"I see," Victor said.

"They say she haunts the Honeymoon Suite to this day, torturing men in their sleep the same way she tortured Logan Thomas. Karen and I . . . " His hand reached out across the breakfast table to clasp his girlfriend's. "We've tried to reserve the Honeymoon Suite a few times, but we can never quite catch it. She's one of only two we haven't seen."

Victor frowned. "Only two?"

This time it was Karen who addressed him, speaking in a tiny, flat voice. "The only ghosts. The only Residents. We've seen all but her and the master of the house."

"This is our seventh visit," Paul said. "Most people have seen the Drowned Maid, but to us she's kind of like the one that got away. But *you've* seen her, haven't you?"

There was such hope in their eyes. Victor could quite happily have snuffed it out. Any other day and he surely would have. But this morning he was still in such a daze. "Yes. I think I did."

The couple practically leapt out of their seats. "Was she beautiful?" Karen asked. "They say she's beautiful."

Victor turned away from her, staring down into his porridge, watching it congeal as it cooled. "I'd say that's a matter of opinion."

John McNee

The rest of the morning was lost in a melancholy fugue. He wandered the hotel grounds aimlessly, trapped in what felt like a bad hangover, unable to quite get his thoughts in order.

Time and again Harry's words came back to him. *You won't find answers here.*

He'd told himself he didn't need answers. But then what was it he had hoped to find in this place? Peace? Serenity? Some small measure of contentment? Such things didn't seem to be an offer. And suppose he had been looking for answers. Suppose what he'd hoped to find was something to help him understand, as he'd told Harry. He'd happily have been denied all that if he could only see Josephine again.

They'd promised nightmares so vivid as to be indistinguishable from reality and the thought hadn't chilled him so much as excited. Josephine haunted his thoughts enough in his waking hours. It made sense that he'd dream of her in this place. And he'd much rather be with her in nightmares than without her in reality.

But he didn't get Josephine, did he? What he got was a date with the Drowned Maid, her diseased tongue twisting in his mouth, her tentacle fingers cutting through his skin. Vivid, yes, but more than that. The pain felt real. The violation felt real.

He didn't know what it was that he'd experienced. Paul and Karen were clearly fantasists. He didn't share their childish delusions about poltergeists, but he didn't believe the visions were mere dreams. Something else was at work in this place.

Something else . . .

He could feel eyes on him as the thought crystallised and he snapped his head towards the first floor window as a figure shifted out of view. Victor stood in the garden, just beyond the hedges. It didn't take him more than a moment to figure out the geography and realise the window at which he was staring belonged to the Library Suite. The brunette.

He sighed, suddenly wanting to be very far away from the hotel, its ghostly attractions and peculiar patrons. There was a temptation to phone Harry, get him back, and tell him, "It's not what I thought it was. Let's just go home." The problem with that was one of his own making. He'd left his phone behind and didn't know Harry's number. He didn't care for the idea of hanging around in the bar all day in case he phoned. And he was a grown man, after all. If he wanted to leave he could just leave. He didn't need to be babysat. He could do what he damn well pleased.

When he thought of things in those terms, the idea of giving in made him angry.

Still in a mood to revolt, though not quite ready to admit defeat, he marched down to the loch, glanced around its edges, then started south, kicking his way through the black pebbles. He buttoned his coat as the breeze picked up and pressed on, hills to his left, the water on his right, and the Ballador behind him, receding slowly into the distance.

Gia stood with her back flat against the wall, silently cursing her own foolishness.

She'd been watching Victor as he wandered, making a circuitous loop of the hedgerows and oak tree. She was at once fascinated and bored, telling herself, *See? He's just a sad old man. Just like any other man. Nothing remarkable about him.*

She said it and repeated it, but couldn't quite make herself believe it, though he did nothing to suggest he was anything else. When finally, like downwind prey catching the scent of a predator, he snapped his head round towards her, she panicked, lurching to the side of the window and throwing herself against the wall.

It was farcical. What did she think would happen if he saw her? What could he do? What possible reason did she have to hide? And yet she clung on, counting down the seconds until she was sure he must have moved away, and even then giving the most tentative peek she could, crouching down and slowly inching her head above the windowsill, to make sure.

When she'd confirmed it, she raised herself back up to her full height, and returned to the dining table, where her laptop sat open, casually displaying the contents of his Wikipedia page:

> Victor Teversham (born October 7, 1939) is an Australian businessman and philanthropist. Born in Kogarah, a southern suburb of Sydney, he is the co-founder, chairman of the board and chief executive officer of Teversham Holdings. Originally involved exclusively in property and retail, Teversham's broad interests eventually prompted the investment in and acquisition of numerous firms dealing in electronics, pharmaceuticals, shipping, oil refining, commodity trading, media and more.

The entry continued for another two thousand words, detailing most of his major battles and triumphs, noting all the awards he and his company had won, his placing in the *Sunday Times Rich List* and recent, surprising appearance in *TIME* magazine's "100 Most Influential."

However, under the heading "Controversies" was only a scant three sentences giving a vague list of public problems he'd quickly overcome. Perhaps most tellingly, the only mention of his wife was limited to a single sentence under "Personal Life:" *Married to his wife Josephine from 2001 until her death in 2015.*

A quick search online dug up a lot more dirt than he and his shareholders might have wished. Questionable business practices, law suits, public battles with former partners, even the occasional criminal investigation (which, of course, led to nothing). There were innumerable blogs from which to choose detailing all of the man's most hateful crimes against humanity (some clearly imagined, others which were undeniably true) along with conspiracy theories about his involvement in everything from providing weapons technology to third world dictatorships, to suppressing cancer treatments for profit and—pushing things almost too far for Gia's tastes—plotting the murder of his wife to make it look like a suicide.

She had been up all the night and most of the morning reviewing her subject. Though she hadn't read enough to call herself an expert, she now knew an awful lot about the man. At least it proved that he *was* a man. Nothing more. A man of some celebrity, some renown, and, with the events of recent months, some cause to have appeared on televisions and newspapers across the western world.

Gia didn't watch the news and didn't recall seeing him before. But she knew she must have. *Must* have. It made sound, logical sense, even if part of her resolutely refused to believe it. The coincidence was still too great.

Victor returned as night was falling.

Pink Lipstick stood in the garden. He was dressed in an obscenely ugly violet suit and smoking a black cigarette. He gave an over-elaborate flourish with his hand by way of greeting as Victor approached. Victor ignored him and continued into the lobby.

Mrs Dempsey was behind the front desk. "Good evening, Mr Teversham," she beamed. "Been anywhere nice?"

"Just out for a stroll," he said, rubbing his hands together. The warmth of the lobby had made him realise how cold it had been outside. "Stopped off at a little pub down the way there, had lunch, came back."

Her brow creased. "Which pub?"

"Oh, I don't know," he said, struggling to remember the name. "The Old Wall or something."

The frown deepened. "The Auld Well?"

"Yes, that was it."

"That's almost ten miles away."

He blinked. It really hadn't seemed like that far, but when he thought it over he realised she was probably right. "Yes. I suppose it was."

She grinned. "You walked almost twenty miles? And without your cane?"

Foolish as it must have appeared to her, he actually glanced down at his left hand, saw the walking cane wasn't there, and remembered he'd left it in the suite when he came down for breakfast in the morning. "Yes. I suppose I did."

"The restorative powers of the highland air, perhaps. You must be exhausted."

"Yes." He wasn't. "I am feeling quite tired, now that you mention it." He felt fine. "Though the prospect of getting forty winks doesn't exactly fill me with joy."

"Ah. I did warn you."

"You did indeed."

"They do say the experience improves the second time around."

"Improves? In what way?"

She shrugged. "I couldn't say, never having gone through it myself. If you really didn't want to go through it again—and I can completely understand that—I could offer you one of the rooms at the rear of the house? We have a couple free at the moment and they tend to be free from any ghostly activity."

"Is that what the dreams are? Ghosts?"

"Most people seem to think so," she said. "I don't know. I wouldn't like to speculate."

"Not hallucinogenics in the food? Or psychotropic gases pumped into the rooms?"

Her expression hardened. "To that I can categorically state *no*."

He leaned forward across the desk, letting a trace of

contempt creep into his voice. "I must say I find it surprising that the hotel's owners and staff should show so little interest in the origins of their quaint little phenomena."

She didn't step away, but did lean back, putting a little more distance between them. "I think there are just some things that can't be explained, Mr Teversham."

"But has anyone even tried? Scientists? Professionals? Anyone with any genuine experience with this sort of thing?"

She shook her head quickly. "No. I don't think the owners would ever allow anything like that."

"No, I suppose not." He sneered. "Why take the risk that they might actually discover the cause, right? You wouldn't want to jeopardise your precious little tourist attraction for the sake of something as frivolous as scientific curiosity. Better to wallow in ignorance and let the cash keep flowing in from the delusional and downright deranged. I can appreciate that, from a businessman's perspective. I can."

She was quiet a moment, apparently waiting until she was sure his little rant was over with, then asked, "Do you want me to have that other room arranged for you?"

He sighed as he straightened up. "No. I'm perfectly happy where I am. Looking forward to a good night's sleep. I'm getting a taste for it now." He strolled away from the desk and started up the stairs. When he was halfway up he turned his head over his shoulder and called back, "Bring on round two, that's what I say! Show me your worst!"

Thorn was the name of a desperately modern piano bar in Glasgow city centre—all chrome, glass, and faux sophistication. It was very popular.

Harry fought his way through the crowd to reach someone who looked like they worked there, gave his own name and asked to speak to Mr Basra. Then, just in case it sped things along, he added, "I work for Victor Teversham." He was directed to an empty corner booth where he sat and waited as the piano player ploughed doggedly through a medley of hits by Billy Joel.

The man who eventually came out to meet him was a middle-aged Indian with stylishly groomed facial hair, wearing a designer suit over a striped black, orange, and pink shirt. He looked right at home. "Something to drink?" he asked, shaking Harry's hand as he motioned to a waitress.

"Sure," Harry said, for the sake of politeness. "Just a scotch on the rocks."

Basra grinned. "On the rocks! You Americans . . . " He made a big show of ordering two glasses of something very rare and very expensive, and then took a seat. "Will Mr Teversham be joining us?"

"No. He's a little preoccupied at the moment, as I'm sure you can imagine."

"Ah, yes." Basra nodded solemnly. "Of course. Bad business. A terrible business."

"I'm currently handling most of his affairs."

"Of course. Well, whatever I can help you with. Is it Thorn

in particular that you were interested in? I could show you around."

Harry shook his head. "I was actually searching for some information about the Ballador House Hotel."

"Ah." Basra's suddenly sheepish smile was full of meaning. "Unfortunately, I no longer own that property. Unfortunately for *you*, that is. Fortunate for me. I'm much happier where I am now. And if you—or Mr Teversham—are looking to purchase I would strongly advise you against it."

"The current owners seem to be doing okay." Harry nodded to the waitress as the drinks arrived. "I was up there just yesterday. Looked like they were doing good business."

"Mmmm. I heard something along those lines. Not that I really keep tabs, but I'd heard they'd managed to turn things to their advantage. And good for them, I suppose. I'd never have imagined there was a demand for such things. But I still wouldn't want to be a part of it." He raised his glass. "Cheers."

"Cheers," Harry answered and tilted his own glass to his lips. Tasted like any other whisky to him.

Basra took a sip, licked his lips and frowned. "Why, may I ask, are you interested in the Ballador? How did you even hear I'd owned it?"

Harry reached into the inside pocket of his coat, produced his copy of 'The History of Ballador House' and passed it across. A pink Post-it note marked the relevant page, on which this passage was highlighted:

. . . *The house sat empty for decades until 1988, when it was purchased by entrepreneur Baldev Basra, who harboured dreams of turning it into a grand country hotel. However, following innumerable ghostly visitations, those plans floundered and were eventually abandoned. Mr Basra finally sold the property a decade later to the current proprietors.*

"Bastards," Basra said and reached again for his glass. "I never agreed to them printing my name in this. They never even asked my permission."

"But is that true what it says?" Harry asked. "The part about ghostly visitations."

"Sort of." Basra flipped quickly through the book. "Is that the only time they mention me in this?"

Harry nodded.

"Bastards." He leaned forward, anger clear in his voice. "You know, I made that place what it is. It was my money, my development. Years spent on the restoration, the extension, making the whole site fit for purpose. If they're going to mention me the least they could do is give me my due credit. But all anyone wants to talk about is the nightmares. They're the reason I had to sell, why it took so long . . . why it cost me such a fortune."

"So you definitely experienced them? They aren't something the current owners dreamed up?"

"I wish." Basra rolled his eyes and took another drink. "No, they're real. Every single night. After I bought the place I would travel up there to tour the building with members of the development team. Sometimes it was cheaper and easier for me to spend the night there, so I did. But I had these horrible dreams. Have you stayed there?"

Harry shook his head.

"Don't. Trust me on this. You really mustn't. It's just as awful as they say. At first I thought it was me. You would, wouldn't you? And it made sense. Sleeping alone in a spooky, abandoned old house, of course I was going to have nightmares, right? But then once the main development of the old house was complete and we were able to move on to the extension, I let the builders sleep in the hotel. Again . . . cheaper and easier. And every last one of them had nightmares."

"It doesn't seem possible," Harry said. "The last few days I've been searching online trying to find another place anywhere in the world that claims to do what the Ballador does. Near as I can tell there aren't any."

"Good," Basra said and raised his glass. "That gives me some comfort."

Prince of Nightmares

Harry smiled and sat back in his seat. "Y'know, looking at it logically—and don't take this the wrong way—but speaking from a strictly business perspective, it would make a lot more sense to me if the current owners paid a little over the asking price on condition that you tell this story to anyone who came asking."

Basra's thick eyebrows crept up his forehead. "You don't believe me?"

Harry's smile broadened into a tension-inspired grin. "I struggle with the whole conceit."

Basra pursed his lips and nodded, then stabbed his finger at the table. "Point one. The current owners paid *well* below the asking price. Like the book says, I wanted to run a hotel. I didn't want to sell it, but when the . . . problems emerged, I decided I had to. I couldn't imagine anyone wanting to pay money to sleep in a hotel where they suffered nightmares every night. Maybe that shows my lack of vision, but it went double for most of the potential buyers who only had to ask around to find out why I wanted rid of it. It took years to find anyone willing to take it off my hands." His finger stabbed the table again. "Point two. I *still* have nightmares."

Harry raised an eyebrow. "Really?"

Basra nodded and bowed his head towards his glass. "Not every night. Only sometimes. So I suppose they might really be mine. But they don't *feel* like mine any more than the others. And sometimes I have to wonder if I just spent a little too long in that fucking house." At that, he put the whisky to his lips and drained the glass.

Harry watched him, going through everything he'd been told in his head, trying to make some sense of the tale and arriving back at the same old thought. "It just doesn't seem possible."

Basra frowned. "Remind me again what your interest is in this?"

Harry didn't want to divulge the details, so kept things simple. "It's part of a puzzle. I'm just trying to figure it out."

Basra smiled sadly. "I don't suppose I've been much help, have I?"

Harry sighed. "Not really."

"And yet," Basra's hand crept towards the book. "Perhaps I can provide you with something." He picked it up and turned to the page Harry had shown him. "Here. Where it says about the hotel sitting empty from 1945 to 1988. That's not true."

Harry sat up. "It's not?"

Basra shook his head slowly. "The first time I walked into that building was the first time anyone had been inside for years. I'm sure of that. But 1945 is a stretch. Touring the rooms, we found bunks, clothes, boxes of books and old albums, even posters of Bob Dylan and The Doors on the walls." He smiled, letting the implication sink in. "Unquestionably, my American friend, there was an unknown period when a great many people lived there, then left in a terrible hurry."

A few hours before Josephine Teversham killed herself, she had dined with Victor in the restaurant of their hotel. It was a large, high-ceilinged room with chandeliers and potted plants, opulently decorated in cream and gold, but for Victor, after a while, all hotel restaurants looked alike.

He was seated first, at a table in the middle of the floor. Josephine was still up in the room, making herself perfect, but had told him to go down without her, knowing his views around punctuality and satisfied that he would order something for her. He always ordered for her. It spared her the embarrassment of having to take out her reading glasses to see the menu.

For Victor, passing the time without his wife was no difficulty. He'd been enduring frantic calls from Edward all day. Even as he was seated and presented with a menu, he still had the phone pressed against his ear. "You'll have to say that again, Ed. And talk a little louder, would you? It's a bad line."

"I said David Walker is holding out. At FBX."

"Walker? Worthless little shit. As though he hasn't accrued enough in his pension pot."

"He's claiming it's a matter of conscience."

"Conscience?" Victor laughed. "If that's all he's worried about, just point him in the direction of a few more cock-hungry rent-boys. I'm sure he'll soon feel better about himself." He was suddenly aware of the waiter shifting awkwardly at his shoulder and placed his hand over the

John McNee

phone. "Won't be a moment," he said, and then put it back to his ear. "Did you hear that Ed? Ed!"

The voice on the line was tinny, slightly distorted. "Hang on, I'm just writing it down. Did you say dick-hungry or cock-hungry?"

"Let me do the fucking jokes, Ed. Just call me back when you've got his name on the dotted line." No reply. "Ed?"

" . . . es . . . Yes, I'm . . . ill . . . here . . . "

"Just call me back, okay?"

" . . . most . . . air . . . "

"What was that?"

" . . . So . . . ose . . . You're all . . . there . . . "

"I'm hanging up, Ed," he said, and did. "You were going to say something?" he asked the waiter.

"Yes," the young man said, as meekly as he was able. "Would you like to order something to drink?"

"Yes, all right. I'll just have a ginger ale for now. No ice. And . . . " The waiter nodded curtly and sped off in the direction of the bar, before Victor could order a drink for Josie. Evidently, he'd concluded that he was dining alone. Victor glowered after him, irritated by the implied slight. He comforted himself by calculating in his head the size of the tip the kid wouldn't be getting.

His phone rang. "Hello? Ed?"

"Victor. Victor, listen to me." The voice was distant, unrecognisable.

"Who is this? Hello?"

"Victor, you're close. So close. You're almost there, but you've got to come a little bit further." Muffled, whispered. He couldn't even tell if it was male or female.

"Talk sense," he said. "Who am I speaking to?"

"This is the wrong room, Victor. Can y . . . stand me?" Again, the line began to crumble. "Y . . . close. But it's n . . . the ri . . . room . . . "

"Hello?" Victor barked. "Hello!"

Nothing but static. He hung up, dropping the phone on

the table as his waiter set down a glass of ginger ale. "Everything all right, sir?"

"Yes," Victor answered, without thinking. "No. You didn't let me order a drink for my wife."

The waiter was confused. "Your wife?"

Victor sighed. The boy was dim, no doubt about it. "Yes. My wife."

"Sorry. I was sure you'd checked in alone."

This was turning into more of a conversation than Victor would have liked. He turned in his chair to give the boy the full benefit of his intimidating gaze. He very rarely made eye contact with waiters, but this seemed like one of those occasions.

His mind went blank when he got his first good look at the kid. Something about his bleach-blond hair. The faux silver trinket glistening in his eyebrow. It wasn't right. "Sir?"

Victor's mouth opened and closed, but no sound emerged. He glanced over his shoulder to the next table and saw the diner—a tanned man with dyed black hair and pink lips. He stared back, smiling. At the table across from him was a young brunette in a short satin nightdress. She sat with her head in her hands, staring sadly at an uneaten sandwich.

"Sir?"

Victor looked across the room to the table on his right, where Paul and Karen were giggling over some inane private joke.

"Is there a problem here?" asked Mrs Dempsey. Victor turned as the manager approached with a look of tired concern evident on her face.

"I . . . don't know," the waiter answered.

"Mr Teversham?"

Victor didn't understand what was happening. He felt listless, adrift. "My . . . wife . . . " he wheezed.

Mrs Dempsey turned her ear towards him. "I'm sorry, what was that?"

Victor raised a quivering finger, pointing it over his head. "My wife . . . She's here. She's upstairs."

Mrs Dempsey winced, sharing a conspiratorial glance with the waiter, then said, "I shouldn't think so, no."

There was a sound like gunfire. A single pistol crack, echoing all around, and Victor was on his feet and moving, suddenly six floors up and running—in a slow way—down the corridor. People were gathered outside his room. Security guards with radios at their lips and curious guests clutching the collars of their luxury bathrobes tight about their necks.

Victor brushed them all aside—they fell away like plastic figurines—and continued into the room, throwing out his hand to the bathroom door. It was unlocked, clicking open at his touch. Josie's name was on his lips, but he never got it out. The smell choked his words—burnt cordite and something more. He pressed on, into the memory, inching around the door and into the bathroom, stretching out his hand to the drawn shower curtain.

It was a kind of inevitability, rather than urgency that motivated him to pull it back, exposing the tub and its contents to his tearful eyes.

It was empty. Clean. Not even a spider.

He stepped back, scanned the room in confusion and caught sight of the note, scrawled across the mirror in her lipstick. *So close. You're almost there.*

He stared at the words a long time, until eventually he looked past them and saw the man behind. His own eyes stared back. His own face, yet it didn't have the feel of a reflection. It looked more like imitation—a plastic-coated waxwork, glistening beneath the bathroom's lights. He felt like he was staring into the eyes of a void man, a vacant, hollow shell.

It made him sad to see.

"A man devoid of a soul," he said, and watched the waxwork lips moving in time with his own. They kept moving after he finished speaking, and he *knew* what they were saying, but was relieved that they made no sound. He didn't want to hear that.

In a moment he was moving again, gliding across the darkness, the dream carrying him where it wished, back out into the corridor, which had warped itself across time and space into the top floor of the Ballador House Hotel.

The doors to each room were open and he graced them in turn.

The first was cold, lit from within by a pale fire's light and cursed by an icy wind, whipping flecks of frost into his face. He halted and blinked, his eyes adjusting to the sudden brightness. When at last he looked around, he found he was standing on the edge of a crystal cliff. A step forward meant a sheer one-mile drop—a tumbling, terrifying plummet to a sudden, violent death on the glittering rocks below.

The cliff face was a wall of jagged glass, a moulded mountain of broken bottles. The glass on which Victor stood was rounded and smooth, but all he saw below him were shattered edges like blades, concentrated in lacerating layers one upon the next upon the next, all the way down and across. He also saw a woman trying to climb it.

Blonde. Forties maybe, though it was hard to tell. She was naked and covered in blood. Old blood—brown and black, dried and crusted. New blood—richly red and pouring down her limbs in thick streams. She was just a foot or so below him, very close to the top, but so hideously ruined by her climb that she seemed unable to progress.

Cuts littered her body, varying widely in depth and degree. Some were simple nicks, the blood around them congealing almost in the instant they opened up. Some—like those on her feet and arms—went so deep they cut through to the bone, red flesh and skin hanging from them in ragged loops and clumps.

Clearly she was in agony, yet she pressed on, trying to pull herself up by pinching the flat sides of a shard with fingers already peeled back to bloody stumps. Seeing Victor through eyes bleary with tears, she reached her other arm up, stretching out her hand towards him. "Help," she begged, through a mouth of bubbling saliva. "Please . . . help me."

Victor stared at her massacred arm and the strips of flayed skin that curled away from it, flapping in the breeze. He wondered if he took her hand and pulled, whether the skin would just slide off in a single piece, like a long, velvet glove.

Whatever the risks, she was clearly more than keen, stretching every muscle in her body up towards him, even as the effort caused her to lean into the wall, its razor points piercing her breasts and belly. "Help me!"

Victor had been letting other forces guide him for a while, moving him from one floor to the next, one room to the next, one reality to another. He'd been a passive observer, but it occurred to him now that whatever energies had been manipulating him had gone, receding into the shadows, allowing him complete control of his mind and body to do with what he wished.

"Help! Please! Help!"

After a moment's hesitation, he inched forward to the very edge, crouched down and offered his arm. "Here," he said. "Come on."

She put her mangled hand in his, wincing as he squeezed and hot blood spurted out between his fingers. He pulled as she released her other hand's grip, lifting her feet away from the intersecting blades of glass, all coated in liquid red.

He strained, heaving her up to the edge, watching the mingling expressions of elation and suffering on her blood-smeared face.

Then, when she was close enough, he gave her a hard kick to the chest, opened his hand and sent her flying away from the cliff, plummeting into oblivion.

She screamed all the way down.

He lay breathless, sprawled out on the glass, grinning as

he listened to the awful noise she made, then clambered back onto his feet and continued into the next room.

Here was darkness and blood. Fire and pain. The wails of the tortured multitudes.

He was aware of phantoms everywhere. A shadow army of unidentifiable creatures whirled about him, excited by his presence. They were a blurry, black cacophony, innumerable and inhuman, but he could see none of them clearly. Whenever he tried to get one in his sights it skittered out of his vision. The clearest evidence of their existence were the marks they left on their victims.

A man and woman were splayed out in the middle of the room. The vaguely rectangular shape on which they lay may once have been a bed, but was now stained by so much blood, oil, meat, and misery that it was impossible to tell.

Victor's hosts had already finished with the woman. The room was a mutilation factory and they'd made her part of the machine, amputating her limbs and securing her in place with iron bolts. Great lengths of metal cable were fed into her mouth, exploding out of open wounds and other leaking orifices. Her fresh blood kept the mechanism lubricated. Any number of the things they'd done should have been enough to kill her, but she was alive and awake, suffering through the torture. Her eyes rolled around as Victor approached, stretching wide when she recognised him. Only then did he realise it was Karen.

Paul was crouched next to her, strapped to the bed and failing to fight off his aggressors. They drove a nail through the palm of his free hand and twisted it. He tried to wrestle it out of their grip, and they snapped the wrist, their small teeth gnawing on his broken fingers.

One of them had already gone to work on his face, carving his cheeks open, slicing off his eyelids, cutting crosses into the white flesh of his left eye.

It looked like he was trying not to scream, trying not to

open his mouth, trying not to let them get at his tongue. Now though, grasping fingers tore away his lips and tried to force their way between his teeth. He held fast, clenching as hard as he could, till the powerful blow of a hammer shattered his incisors. Blood spurted from his throat. Metal implements pried his mouth open as fingers forced their way in, tearing through what remained of his cheeks, to grab a good hold of his jaw and rip it free from the rest of his head, before a blade pierced his tongue and sliced it in two. A bony hand grabbed the hairs on what was left of his scalp and raised his head up, so that his bloody throat was exposed.

His tormentors, their bodies like smoke, peeled back now and thrust a heavy stone jug into Victor's hands. He stared down at it, then at Paul, feeling the encouragement from all sides.

Paul looked up with what remained of his eyes, straining to focus through the tears and the blood and the pain. All he could see of the man in front of him was a dark figure approaching with some kind of container. He couldn't see what it held, but he could smell the contents. He could feel the heat on his mutilated face.

He must have known it was hot tar, because he screamed then, in the moment before Victor tipped the jug forward and choked him.

He didn't go into the third room, only lingered in the doorway.

It was dark, darker than the rest, but lit intermittently by schizophrenic flashes of electricity. In those moments he could see the outlines of the room's occupants, highlighted in fizzing blue. A little bit here, a little over there. Watching and waiting in silence, he was slowly able to put the images together, forming a gruesome jigsaw puzzle.

Every available inch of the ceiling had been pierced with a black metal hook. From these hung endless yards of steel chains, looping and intersecting, creating supports for fat lumps of dead flesh. It was impossible to tell whether they were human or animal. They were dead, bled dry and rotting in their chain hammocks. The floor was littered with stray pieces of meat, limbs, heads, and bones. Nothing moved, not even the figure in the far corner, who regarded Victor with quiet, curious eyes.

Whatever it was, it had the vague appearance of a man composed of roiling thunderstorms. A vast silhouette of molten black shot through with involuntary flash-pops of lightning. This creature was the source of the blue flashes, the only light in the room. He was also, Victor surmised, the one responsible for the countless dead scattered between them.

They stared at each other across the bodies and though nobody moved and nothing was said, Victor deduced that the figure wished for him to enter, to join him in the darkness, among the chains and rotting flesh.

He further deduced that if he crossed the threshold he'd shortly join the others on the floor, his own body shredded into unrecognisable matter, his own blood darkening the walls.

Being reluctant to so indulge the room's occupant, he took a step back and turned away.

"So close. You're almost there."

Back in the corridor now, on the landing, on the top floor of the Ballador, and heading down. His hand gripped the banister as he took to the carpeted stairs. He knew his destination now. It was as obvious as could be.

"You're close. But it's not the right room."

The voice whispered to him through the wall, accruing clarity with every step he took. He was close now. It wasn't only the voice telling him that. He felt it in his veins. So close.

He descended to the first floor landing and passed the door to his own suite, feeling the weight in his bare feet as he planted them on the rug. He wasn't gliding any more. This was a determined gait. He swung about and continued in the direction of the Library Suite and its heavy oak door.

"Almost there," said the voice.

"Mr Teversham?" said another.

He staggered towards the door, into the warming embrace of urgent shadows, coiling their way around him, pulling him in. A voice called out to him from the other side. A young woman, gasping and crying from the pleasure and the pain. She called his name.

"Mr Teversham?"

So close.

He reached out and gripped the handle.

Almost there.

"Mr Teversham!"

A hand snatched at his arm and tugged him back. Another struck his cheek, shattering the illusion. The voices died out. Shadows receded, twisting away into the ether.

He blinked. "What?"

"Mr Teversham, wake up!" The hand struck again, a light slap on the face, just enough to shock him out of the dream.

"Yes! What?" He swatted the hand away and stumbled back, but was caught by the front of his pyjama top and pulled forward. "What's happening?" He blinked again, glanced around. He was standing on the landing outside the Library Suite in wrinkled nightwear, his skin clammy with sweat. Mrs Dempsey had a hold of him.

"It's nothing," she said, lifting his arm and putting it around her. "It's quite all right."

"I don't understand," he said. "What am I doing here?"

"Don't fret," she said, patting his hand where it sat limply on her shoulder. She led him back across the landing to his own suite and the door he'd left ajar in his wake. "You were only sleepwalking."

Harry lay on the bed in his nondescript room in a nondescript hotel on the outskirts of Glasgow. The television was on—some current affairs show where a stern-looking woman was barking questions at a sweaty, grinning man in a grey suit—but he wasn't watching it. He had 'The History of Ballador House' in his hands again, open at the chapter titled 'Ghosts of Ballador House'.

There were six pages in the chapter, and on each page a number of entries describing each of the hotel's supposed poltergeists were accompanied by sloppy illustrations.

He'd read the guidebook cover to cover maybe a dozen times, but kept finding himself drawn back to this chapter, eyes glancing across the names of the spectres: The Drowned Maid, The Ferryman, The Black Worm . . . The way the book told it, there were more ghosts in the Ballador than days in the week. He lingered on one entry, The Crystal Mistress.

"Crystal Mistress," he murmured, wanting to hear the way it sounded out loud. "Crystal Mistress." It was a bad name, he decided.

He read on:

> *Not to be confused with the Drowned Maid, the Crystal Mistress most commonly appears to guests on the top floor and generates dreams of a very different nature indeed. There is general consensus among researchers that the spirit is that of Jane Dawson, a young cousin of the Baileys, who came to stay with the family in the winter of 1890, while*

suffering from an acute bout of chronic hysteria. According to the letters of Sir William Bailey, it was during one especially violent night time episode that Miss Dawson fled the house, running into the hills. Though a search party was formed, she was never found, and was presumed to have frozen to death somewhere in the woods.

Those who have seen the Crystal Mistress describe a still, silent and beautiful young woman, her body translucent, like sheet ice. Other guests insist she has greatly influenced their dreams, while failing to make a personal appearance. The nightmares with which she is associated focus on images of frost, snow, and shattered glass.

Beside the entry was a blotchy illustration that looked like an inverted, negative photocopy of the Drowned Maid's picture. That had shown the black outline of a left-facing woman on a white background, while this showed the white outline of a right-facing woman on a black background. "Not to be confused" indeed.

The illustrations for the rest weren't much better. The Master of the House, described only as "a man in a dark suit" was featured in no better detail than the average decal on a gents' toilet door. The Swarm was even worse—a spattering of black dots devoid of form or purpose, as though someone had sneezed ink on the page.

Harry yawned and felt tears spring to his eyes—a sure sign that he was past the point of exhaustion—yet felt his fingers flicking through the pages back to the table of contents. The family names of most of the Ballador's residents throughout its history were scattered across the chapter titles: Dunn (1820-1855), Thomas (1855-1868), Bailey (1869-1910), McLoughty (1910-1945).

The list was incomplete. Harry knew that. Baldev Basra had confirmed it. But what concerned him almost equally

Prince of Nightmares

was that no matter how many times he read through the book, he still couldn't figure out when the nightmares or visitations or sightings were supposed to have begun. In most respects, the book was a mine of information, yet in this most critical aspect it had failed him. Again, fearing he'd missed something, he turned to the opening chapter.

In 1820, Mrs Emma Dunn, wife of Dr. Adam Dunn (a London physician) bought the property of Ballador. Dr. Dunn liked the name of Ballador and gave it to the house that he built on the land his wife had bought. He died shortly after the house was built in 1853 and theories postulate his own spectre haunts the library in the form of the Master of the House.

Harry closed the book, deciding he was much too tired to continue. He dropped it on the bedside table, turned out the light and lay in the dark, wondering what dreams Victor might be having.

10

"Please don't be embarrassed." Mrs Dempsey was on her knees, lighting a fire in the hearth. It was the third or fourth time she'd said this since finding Victor in the hallway.

He sat on the couch, facing toward her, but staring at the wall. "No," he said. "No sense in that. I suppose I should just get used to it. Getting to that age where wandering about in your pyjamas is the thin end of the wedge. Soon I'll be forgetting my own name and shitting the bed. No sense in being embarrassed about anything."

"Oh, hush now," she chided, rising slowly and awkwardly to her feet. "That's all decades ahead. You're a fine figure of a man."

"For my age, sure."

"For *any* age. You walked twenty miles today, remember? How are you feeling after that, by the way? Any aches and pains?"

"No," Victor answered, truthfully. "Nothing beyond the usual."

She grinned. "Well there you go, you see? It's not every man who could walk twenty miles in a day and feel none the worse for wear. Like I said, the sleepwalking is nothing to do with age. It just happens here sometimes. Another symptom of our 'quaint little phenomena.' That was what you called it, right?"

Victor cringed. "Something like that. I . . . I should apologise for the way I spoke to you earlier."

She waved it away. "Think nothing of it."

"I feel like I've been doing an awful lot of apologising to you since I've been here."

"And it's only your second night!" She laughed.

There was a knock at the door and Mrs Dempsey answered it. The waiter with the pierced eyebrow entered with a tray of drinks and brought them over to the coffee table.

"Hot cocoa," Mrs Dempsey said. "Do you a power of good. Thank you, Dennis."

The waiter nodded and made his way out. Mrs Dempsey closed the door behind him.

"Thank you," said Victor, sounding confused. "I . . . didn't even notice you order it."

Something about the way she smiled reminded him of his mother. Sympathy and experience. "You're still half-asleep, aren't you?"

He shrugged. "I really don't know. It sounds a dangerous state to be in, in this place."

"Somewhat." She sat down in the armchair on his right and reached for one of the cups. "Do you remember what you were dreaming about, when I shook you out of it?"

He nodded. "I felt this . . . overriding compulsion to get beyond that door. Like I knew there was someone waiting for me on the other side."

Mrs Dempsey raised an eyebrow. "The French girl? Mr Teversham, I didn't realise it was *that* sort of dream."

"Hardly." He rubbed his eyes and glanced around the room, searching for a clock. "What time is it?"

"A little after midnight," she answered between sips. "The witching hour."

"I can't have been asleep very long." He yawned, and then leaned towards her, squinting in the low lamplight. "Mrs Dempsey, are you *always* here?"

Her eyes widened ever so slightly, and she smiled. "Why yes, Mr Teversham. I'm the Phantom Manageress, cursed to roam these halls for eternity. Didn't you read your guidebook?"

He sighed. "It was a stupid question. Forgive me. My head . . . "

She laughed. "I'm the evening manager, seeing as you hadn't figured it out. Very reasonable hours. There's a day manager. Pay a wee bit more attention tomorrow morning and you might notice him."

"It's dumb, I know. It just felt like you and that boy were the only members of staff I'd seen."

"Dennis? Well, he does work longer hours than I do, it has to be said. You likely would see a lot of him."

"Even in my dreams," he said.

"Oh really?" She took another sip of cocoa and set the cup down. "And how are they, your dreams?"

"Vivid," Victor said. "Big as life and twice as ugly, as they say."

Mrs Dempsey shifted in her seat, crossing her legs and clasping her hands in her lap. In just a moment she'd assumed a position that made her appear very much like a consulting psychiatrist. Victor knew that he, slouching in his wrinkled pyjamas, probably appeared very much like an incarcerated mental patient. "Do you mind if I ask you a question?" she said.

He shrugged. "Take your best shot."

She peered at him intently through eyelashes thick with mascara. "Why are you here?"

"Ah," he said, staring at his feet, unwilling to meet her gaze. "I suppose you ask that of all the guests?"

"I don't have to. It's usually written all over their faces. They're looking for a new thrill, an inexplicable experience, something to tell their friends about. The ones who come back turn it into a hobby, like bungee jumping or scuba diving. You don't strike me as a thrill-seeker."

"No," he admitted "But . . . What *do* you know about me?"

She took a breath, shrugging with her eyebrows. "Not a lot. About as much as most people. I know you're very rich. I've heard of your company and the more famous stories associated with it. I'd seen your face on the news before you checked in."

"You know what happened to my wife?"

She hesitated a moment, then nodded. "She died."

Victor cringed and raised a finger, as though making a point of order. "She didn't *die*. She *killed* herself. Shot herself in the bathroom of a Sydney hotel, which was a tricky thing for her to do, when you think about it. The police say they're still trying to work out where she got the gun, but I doubt they'll ever find out. The point is it couldn't have been a simple thing. We'd been back in the country only a couple of days."

Mrs Dempsey nodded slowly.

"Pills would have been opportunistic," Victor continued. "A razor blade . . . Throwing herself out the window would kill her just as surely if she was overcome by suicidal thoughts in a moment of madness. But a gun? It's like she was deliberately making it difficult for herself, setting herself a challenge with two dozen points of complication, any one of which would have given her the chance to stop, think, and reconsider. And every time she did . . . Every time she did . . . " He paused, his hands open in front of him, eyes roving across them, searching for the words that would let him continue.

It felt very dark in the room now.

"She was determined," he said at last. "For whatever reason, she was committed to killing herself, and to doing so in a way that would actually test that commitment. So you see, she didn't take it lightly. Whatever else you can say about it, it wasn't opportunistic. You understand?"

Mrs Dempsey nodded, though it was almost imperceptible. Her head was a black shadow, framed red in the fireside's glow.

"My problem," said Victor, "quite apart from the question of *why* she killed herself, is that it wasn't the only thing she did that day. And if we conclude from the evidence that her suicide was a careful, considered act by a sane, logical

John McNee

woman, then it stands to reason that anything else she did would be just as considered. Just as logical."

Mrs Dempsey's voice was a whisper in the darkness. "What did she do, Mr Teversham?"

Victor licked his lips. His whole mouth felt dry. "Hours—maybe just minutes—before she killed herself, she went online and made a reservation here. Booked the Library Suite for four nights. In my name." He threw up his hands. "So here I am, seeing it through. It was almost the very last thing she did on this earth. And I can't for the life of me figure out why she did it."

Mrs Dempsey made no movement, but her voice persisted, low and emotionless. "What did you hope to find here?"

"I don't know," Victor said. "I don't know. Just something. Anything to help me understand."

"She wasn't in the habit of booking stays in haunted hotels?"

"No. No, she was not."

"She'd never been here before?"

"Definitely not. Never spoke of it. Never gave any indication that she even knew of its existence. It doesn't make any sense, you see?" He bowed his head into his hands.

"It's quite all right, Mr Teversham. Quite all right."

He remained that way for a while, bent over on the couch, cupping his forehead in his palms, the heels of his hands pressed against his eyes. In the darkness there was only the whisper of the flames in the hearth, the crackle of kindling.

He sighed, lifted his head and slumped back in his seat, but didn't open his eyes. "I don't dream. Not even of Josie. But I'd like to. To be with her for just a little while, talk to her, hold her, just see her. I think I *need* that. Even if it has to be a nightmare."

He opened his eyes to find Mrs Dempsey beside him, perched on the arm of the couch like a gargoyle. The face of an old man leered out from under her helmet of hair, skin powder-white and glistening, eyes and teeth aglow like fluorescent milk.

"Get out." Snarling words through gritted teeth. "Get the fuck out."

It was the face of a corpse.

The masque of death.

She lunged forward, leaning her head towards him as her mouth clicked open, grinning jaw distending into a black chasm, ready to swallow him whole.

Victor shrieked.

. . . and started awake.

He was still on the couch, panting with fright, but otherwise all right. His eyes scanned the room, generously lit by a number of lamps, picking out finer details like the dying embers in the fireplace, the slivers of early-morning light poking through the curtains and the cups of cocoa on the coffee table, his own untouched and stone cold.

Mrs Dempsey was gone. He didn't know what time it was, but could only assume she'd left the room some hours before. He was alone.

Victor took a deep breath, swallowed, and then pulled himself to his feet. Feeling dizzy and still a little queasy from the shock, he stumbled off in the direction of the bathroom, where he would begin the futile business of trying to work out how much of his evening had been real, and how much a dream.

When Gia awoke, just a couple of hours after Victor, she found herself clinging to the end of the bed, her hands seized up like a vulture's talons. She could taste blood in her mouth, but knew there would be none, just as surely as she knew the spots of searing pain on her body would reveal no scars, no bruises, no marks of any kind. That knowledge didn't make her suffering any more slight, nor rinse the taste of iron from her tongue.

Moving slowly for the sake of her tender flesh, she peeled herself from the sheets and manoeuvred into a sitting position. The smell in the room was bad—a lingering soupy musk like the after-scent of strange sex and murder. Her hair and skin felt greasy and sticky at the same time. Sweat on her fingers, sweat in her eyes. She felt almost like there was sweat on her brain, a salty condensation coating the inside of her skull.

Get out, she told herself. *Get the fuck out.*

She shivered suddenly, and then wiped a hand across her face. She stood and staggered to the shower.

Hiking trails led from the rear of the hotel grounds into the hills. Gia asked the kitchen to make her a packed lunch and put it in her rucksack with a couple of bottles of water and a book. She dressed in her most sensible clothes and shoes, tied her hair back and slung the pack over her shoulder, then bounced out of the door and practically jogged up the first two miles.

She wasn't sure, at first, where she was going, but when

she realised the route she was on was leading her up the mountainside, she decided to set her sights on reaching the summit.

It was good to be out. Good to be out of the room and out of the city, fresh air in her lungs and dirt under her feet. The woodland crowding the foothills felt as dense as a rainforest, teeming with wildlife. Rabbits and squirrels, in particular, seemed overly familiar, wandering out into her path and occasionally following along behind. Deer had more sense, and the only one she spotted—a small red hind—darted off through the trees almost the second Gia saw her.

Insects were much too numerous to be ignored. Gia, who'd always harboured a passing interest in entomology, found the clouds of frantic midges as irritating as anyone else would, but the butterflies, beetles, and spiders she encountered never ceased to fascinate. And, when she sat down on a log to rest, she couldn't resist rolling it over to see what curious creatures crawled underneath.

Eventually, the trees thinned out, along with the trail, leaving her trudging up alternately mossy and rocky ground and trying to keep from stumbling into a bog.

She'd hoped to eat lunch at the peak, but three hours in, hunger got the better of her, so she picked a spot of ground that looked dry, dropped onto it and ate. From her position she had a good view of the loch, the forests, and hills surrounding it. There wasn't a person in sight. No boats on the water, no planes in the sky. She knew roughly where the Ballador was, but it was shielded by the trees, as were the roads. Come nightfall, she would likely have been able to see the lights of civilization in the distance, but for the moment she felt able to imagine herself the only person in a hundred mile radius. The only person in the country. The loneliest human being in the world.

The fantasy didn't frighten her so much as intoxicate. For a beautiful few moments, sprawled out in the heather, she felt she could truly breathe.

The sky, though, which had been an ill-tempered shade of grey all day, continued to threaten rain, and Gia felt she better press on before it followed through. So she continued on her way, doggedly maintaining a marching pace even as the slope steepened, eventually becoming so sheer that she was practically crawling on hands and knees the last hundred feet to the summit.

When at last she drew level with the crest and saw nothing beyond but sky, she allowed herself a silent cheer and let a grin spread across her face, proud of herself for making it the whole way.

That grin vanished when she came over the top and saw Victor.

He was sitting on a large, flat rock, turned away from her, staring down into the next valley. Gia's first instinct was to drop onto her stomach and skitter back down the slope, before he even knew she was there. Somehow, she remained standing and, after a few moments' hesitation, summoned up enough courage to make her approach. "Hello?"

He seemed not to hear her, so she tried again.

"Hello!"

This time he raised his head and turned, slowly, squinting at her and waving his hand, by way of tentative greeting.

It was fairly obvious he didn't recognise her, but she very well might not have recognised herself in her pink waterproofs and pony-tail. Victor, for his part, was dressed in tweed and corduroys—not the most practical outfit. As she drew nearer, Gia could see he was also wearing brown brogues, caked in mud, and wasn't carrying a backpack. No supplies of any kind, it looked like. It didn't seem possible that he'd made it to the top of the mountain like that, at his age.

"We're neighbours," she said when they were close enough to talk.

"What's that?" he said.

"Neighbours." She smiled, doing her best to make it look

friendly. The art of politely approaching strangers was something she'd never quite mastered. "At the hotel. You remember? You came to my door?"

"Ah." He did remember. "The Library Suite. Sorry."

"*I'm* sorry," she said. "It was weird. My fault. I didn't know if I was dreaming. I . . . I know that sounds stupid."

"No, not at all." Victor smiled. "I know just what you mean."

He didn't seem in a rush to add anything else. Gia made up her mind to edge a little closer, quickly thinking of something to say before an awkward silence took hold. "So . . . what brings you to the top of the mountain?" For a moment she imagined him being dropped off by private helicopter and had to wonder if it was really such a crazy idea. He could certainly afford it, she knew that much.

"I, um . . . I honestly don't know," he said. "I just started walking, and . . . I don't think it's a mountain. I think it's just a hill."

"Anything above a thousand feet is a mountain, I think." She was certain she'd heard that before.

"This isn't over a thousand feet. Is it?" He seemed slow, dazed, almost sleepy.

"I think it is," she said, almost mimicking his cadence. "Don't you think so?"

He turned away from her, gazing out across the valley again, eyes narrowed, as though he was just figuring out where he was for the first time. "Well, it *could* be, I suppose. It . . . really didn't seem like I'd come that far."

She sat down beside him on the rock. Not too close, but close enough. "It's beautiful," she said, as they both shared the view.

After a minute or so spent in silence, he turned to her and asked, "You're French?"

"I am." She grinned. "Do you speak French?"

"No. No. Not at all." A pause. "First . . . time in Scotland?" His own attempts at small talk were as awkward as hers. It was almost a relief. Endearing in its own way.

"Yes. It's lovely. I feel bad for not making the most of it. I've kept myself so trapped in my room since I arrived. Today I just finally had this urge to get out. Couldn't ignore it."

"Yeah, me too," he said. "Same thing. Had to get out. It's my head, it's just . . . all messed up."

"It'll do that," she said, meaning the hotel. Meaning the dreams.

He turned his head back to face the landscape, but she kept her eyes on him, examining his profile. He didn't look nearly so old as she'd first thought. Certainly, he looked much better in the flesh than in the pictures she'd found on the internet. His jaw looked stronger. His skin seemed tighter, with a better colour to it. Even the baldness didn't seem as pronounced as when he'd appeared at her door, though he was still pretty bald.

"Would you like some chocolate?" she asked, fishing in the pocket of her jacket. "I didn't bring much, but . . . I didn't think there'd be anyone else up here."

He smiled a little sheepishly. "I, uh . . . I wouldn't say no, actually."

She returned the smile, produced a small bar of dark chocolate and broke it in half. "Gia," she said, as she handed him his piece. "That's my name."

"Victor. And thank you."

She could have told him she already knew his name. She could have said she knew *exactly* who he was, had read up on all his achievements, scandals, and personal tragedies. There were a great many things she could have said.

Instead, they sat in silence, watching the shadows of clouds moving across the valley and eating chocolate.

When they were both finished, Victor looked around and nodded. "I suppose it is a mountain. How long do you think it'll take us to get down off this thing?"

She laughed, stood, and held out her hand. "Come on. Let's find out."

Prince of Nightmares

Conversation came a little easier once they were on their way down. They continued to be awkward around each other for a while, speaking in fits and starts, until Victor asked her what she did for a living. Gia didn't go into the finer details, but said she was a dancer, which led to him revealing his patronage of a ballet company in Sydney. Victor Teversham was patron of many things, of course, and Gia's research had told her as much, but she hadn't read about the ballet company, so she was doubly surprised and enthused when he told her.

So they spoke of dance for a while, with Gia leading the discussion. This led inevitably into talk of opera, which they had both studied to some extent, segueing into a conversation about musical genres and artists they actually enjoyed. This, in turn, led them onto the topic of literature, and, somewhat inexplicably, the author Herman Hesse.

Gia, it seemed, had read everything Herman Hesse had ever published and translated into French. Victor couldn't recall if he'd ever read anything by Herman Hesse in his life, but thought he did a pretty good impression of a man who knew what she was talking about. Old men should know old authors, after all. It wouldn't do for him to admit to gaps in his knowledge.

He dropped the "wise old man" act when she started talking about bugs, pointing out every creepy crawly that skittered past them in the woods. Victor couldn't say whether any of what she said was factual or if she was just making it all up. Either way, he was impressed. After a while, he began to suspect that was the whole point. She *wanted* him to be impressed. She wanted to prove to him that she was a lot more than just a pretty face. He didn't know why, but wasn't about to push to find out. It was nice enough, for the time being, just to be in her company.

They reached the end of the trail, emerging into the

grounds of the Ballador, having covered numerous subjects without ever touching upon their most obvious area of common ground. It wasn't that neither of them wanted to talk about the nightmares. Rather, it felt that they'd both made an unspoken pact to hold something back for later.

"You're staying alone," Gia said, as they passed the hedgerows. The garden was empty. No mysterious women. No pink-lipped men.

"I am," Victor said.

"Me too. It's good. I quite like it. Except for mealtimes. I've always hated dining alone. Perhaps, this evening, you'd like to join me?"

12

"You're lucky. Very, very lucky." Gordon Gallan, wide of waist and red of face, grinned from the other side of his desk and waved Harry to a chair. "If you'd called tomorrow I'd have been on a plane halfway to Grenada."

Harry took a look around the office. It looked like it had last been decorated in the early nineties, perhaps last cleaned then as well. The furnishings were cheap, functional, and not what one might expect in the chambers of an Edinburgh estate lawyer. But Harry could tell Gallan was a man who was perfectly happy to work in drudgery as long as he could dine at brasseries every lunch and take six holidays a year to the Caribbean. As with most men in his line of work, he was also more than happy to make room in his busy schedule for envoys of Teversham Holdings, in case they should happen to spill any of that famed wealth on their way out of the premises.

"I want to talk about the McLoughty estate," Harry said, before he'd even sat down.

Gallan frowned slightly, but the grin didn't quite leave his face. "Certainly. Any property in particular?"

"Ballador House."

That did it. "Ah. Well I'm afraid we sold the Ballador many, many years ago. Can't remember the chap's name."

"Baldev Basra," said Harry.

"Was it? Well, in any case, it's sold. There are others in the portfolio."

"Specifically, it's the history of the Ballador I'm interested in."

"I see." Harry could tell the man was trying to calculate whether it was worth his time to continue the conversation. He sat down. "Well ask away. I'll do my best."

"I'm trying to find a little more information on the years from 1945 to 1988."

"Like what?"

"Like . . . well . . . like, *anything*." He smiled. "The only stuff I know I got from the guidebook. Says the McLoughty family vacated in '45 and Basra bought it in '88."

"That's not untrue," Gallan said. "It ceased to be a main residence in '45, but Fergus McLoughty maintained ownership, along with numerous other properties, until his death in '84. I knew Fergus McLoughty, you know. Or at least I met him a couple of times."

"That so?"

Gallan nodded solemnly. "Tragic man. A tragic family. He was a playboy—or something like it—in his day, shirking all responsibilities, mollycoddled by everyone around him, the favourite of his parents, siblings, every aunt, uncle, and maid. Then came the war, which, as with many other families, took a heavy toll. All that wealth and privilege couldn't alter fate. At the end of it he found himself the last in his line, inheriting a fortune far beyond his capabilities to manage. And of course he was crippled, both physically and mentally, unable to sire an heir or manage his estate.

"So Ballador House was too remote for him. He maintained it as a kind of holiday home and moved to the city. All the rest he left to go to rack and ruin. That's why I'm here, still trying to sort through it all today."

Harry nodded in a commiserating sort of way, though he strongly suspected the real reason Gallan was still 'sorting through' the McLoughty estate after almost thirty years was because he was bleeding it dry. "So he still used the house sometimes?"

"On occasion, for a few years, at least. Travelling up there put far too much strain on him towards the end of his life."

"But he'd have known if anyone else was staying there?"

Gallan was quiet for a few moments, staring at Harry without expression. Then he said, "Are you asking me if anyone else stayed there between 1945 and 1988?"

Harry smiled, a little awkwardly. "I, uh . . . I guess so, yeah."

Gallan sighed. "No harm in asking a straight question, you know. Pointless to go all around the houses. The woman you're looking for is called Evelyn Burgess."

Harry frowned, not quite comprehending. "You, uh . . . you're sure?"

"Oh aye," Gallan said. "She was the only one he ever let stay there. She and her lunatic disciples. Don't ask me how she ever talked him into it. For some reason he was convinced if he stuck close to her she'd eventually figure out a way to make him walk again or grant him eternal youth or some other magical shite. He was like that right up till his death. I don't know how she wormed her way into his head but . . . you know what those cults are like. Hang on. I've got her address here somewhere." He opened a drawer in his desk and started rooting around.

Harry sat up. "You're serious?"

Gallan laughed sadly. "You're not the first person to come asking me about Evelyn Burgess, you know." His hand came out of the drawer holding a small, red book. "Here we are," he said, turning to the back page. "Ayrshire address. You'll want to write this down."

13

Victor caught himself whistling in the bathroom. He was shaving, his neck slathered in foam, razor poised just to the left of his Adam's apple. He froze at the sound of a jaunty tune, bouncing off the tiled walls. He raised his eyes from the reflection of his throat, saw his own pursed lips, and realised he was the one making the sound

That was very bad form, he imagined. A recently widowed husband shouldn't be whistling in the depths of his mourning. Certainly not when his wife had perished in such a sudden, violent, haunting manner. In a bathroom.

In his peripheral vision he could see that the shower curtain had once more been drawn across to conceal the bathtub. It had to be the maid's doing, though he couldn't imagine what her angle was. To Victor, it felt unnatural for a shower curtain to be drawn when there was no one behind it . . . presuming there *was* no one behind it.

His hand itched to reach out and pull it back. It was the same impulse he'd have walking into any bathroom and finding it drawn. For some reason, he hadn't noticed it when he'd come in this time. Too wrapped up in thoughts about dinner, Gia, the song . . . what was the song? He'd been whistling a tune he didn't recognise and was now uncertain whether he'd dredged it up from somewhere in the back of his head, overheard, or invented it.

He whistled it a couple more times, but lost the thread after the first couple of phrases. Words. Did it have words?

He closed his eyes and let them come. "I'd rather be . . . da, da, da, da . . . "

When he managed to clear the thoughts from his head and held himself still for a moment, he could almost hear it. An ethereal, half-remembered melody, barely audible through the old Victrola hisses and pops of his subconscious. But it was no good. He got so far, feeling like he was on the verge of an epiphany, like its origin and significance might explode into his thoughts at any second, but then it wriggled away from him like a silverfish and left him standing dumbly in silence.

He blinked, shaking the tatters of the tune from his head and turning his attention back to his reflection. Something in the way his own eyes glanced back at him made him pause. It wasn't an obvious thing. A trick of the light or perceptive failings of a tired, old mind. But for the merest fraction of a second, it had seemed as though he and his reflection were out of synch.

Victor smiled, suddenly imagining himself re-enacting Groucho Marx's mirror routine, putting the figure opposite to the test. His reflection smiled back at him. His teeth, he noticed, were looking whiter than normal. The bags under his eyes seemed to have receded. Something to do with all the rest and recuperation, perhaps.

He finished shaving and went out into the bedroom, closing the door behind him. He left the shower curtain where it was, hoping any ghouls lurking behind would choose to remain where they were for the time being.

He'd chosen to dress simply for dinner. Dark jacket over a white shirt with thick blue stripes. He buttoned the shirt, reached for the cuff links on the dressing table . . . and missed them by an inch. For a moment it was like they were skittering away from him, taking the table, wall, and carpet with them. Like the whole room suddenly stretched outward, an expanding bubble about to burst. Glancing around, Victor felt like he was momentarily looking at everything through the wrong end of a telescope.

Then it stopped. It felt like a listing ship righting itself, reality snapping back into place. And Victor couldn't be sure whether what he'd experienced had been the near disintegration of the universe or a fleeting spell of vertigo.

Taking a little more care this time, he picked up the cuff links, snapped them on, and pulled on his jacket. He checked his reflection again just once more before heading down, doing his best to ignore the strange look it gave him, like it knew something he didn't.

When he saw Gia, Victor immediately regretted not making more of an effort. She wore an elegant dress of deep, dark red that clung to her athletic frame like paint. Her hair was curled and pinned up at one side to show off a dangling earring. Though she'd appeared to him fresh-faced on the hill, she was heavily made-up now. Eyes framed by darkness, crimson lips plumply pronounced against the white of her skin. Deliberately provocative. They'd have called a girl like her "vampish" in his day. She moved like a thin funnel of red smoke when she approached.

"I've such an appetite," she laughed, sliding her arm into his without invitation. "Must be all the exercise."

"Must be," he said, gazing down into her smiling face and for a moment completely unable to think of how to proceed.

Taking the lead, she nodded towards the dining room. "Shall we?"

"Uh, yes," he stammered. "Yes. Let's."

He half-expected heads to turn when they entered the dining room, for everyone to cease their chatter and awkward silence to descend, like something from a film. It didn't happen that way since the restaurant, as usual, was almost empty.

Only one table was occupied by Paul and Karen picking at their plates in miserable silence. Victor nodded to them as he sat down. Karen didn't look up, but Paul shot him a glare that looked at once both furious and fearful. Victor didn't have time to try and interpret it before a man stepped in front of him, obscuring his view. "Good evening." Clipped German tones.

Victor looked up into the face of the pink-lipped man, twisted into an unnatural grin. He wore a three-piece chequered black and red suit that almost perfectly matched the shade of Gia's dress.

"Victor, this is Heinrich Stritzel," she said. "You don't mind if he joins us, do you?"

Victor felt ambushed. His instinct was to turn and flee, but even for a man who'd long ago abandoned concerns with societal graces and embarrassments, that was perhaps a step too far. And he couldn't quite bring himself to abandon the girl. His gaze flickered rapidly from her perfect face to the horrifying waxen features of the man standing over him, pale eyes bulging out of his head.

"No, not at all," he said, in a quiet voice. "The more the merrier."

"*Danke schön.*" Heinrich bowed his head stiffly, but refrained from clicking his heels. He pulled out a chair and sat down, nudging forward, close enough to Victor that their knees were almost touching. "We almost met before, of course," he said, grin still plastered across his face.

"Yes," Victor stated, without inflection.

"I've been hoping for an opportunity to apologise. If I made you uncomfortable, it certainly wasn't my intent. I, of course, recognised you and I suppose I was a little awestruck. A man such as yourself carries with him a certain reputation."

"I do, do I?" Victor glanced at Gia, but her expression was imperceptible.

Heinrich pointed at her and laughed. "Gia, dear sweet thing, hadn't heard of you. I had to tell her all about you. 'Gia,' I said, 'this is a very important man.' All the things you'd done, all the lives you've shaped. Teversham Holdings, oil, media, military hardware. 'As far as some are concerned,'

I said, 'Victor Teversham is the Dark Lord himself.' Tever*shame*, the papers said. Or was it Tever*shambles*?"

"Tever*shame*," Victor stated, as plainly as he could.

"Yes," Heinrich said, happily. "Someone coined that after the KLM landmine scandal. All those poor crippled African children. Of course, you came out of that fairly well in the end, didn't you?"

"I wonder if you bothered to mention any of the good things I've done?" The tension in Victor's voice was pronounced.

"I would have," Heinrich said. "If I could find any!" He exploded into obnoxious laughter.

Gia laughed along with him, in what Victor surmised was part politeness and partly an effort to ease the tension.

He gave a smile false enough to look like a grimace. It was the best he could do. "Are the two of you together?" he asked.

"Oh, my goodness, no." Heinrich laughed. "How fortunate I would be, but no. We're both vacationing alone and so we struck up a kind of companionship. It's important, you see, to have someone to talk to, share your experiences. Couples like them . . . " He waved a hand in the direction of Paul and Karen. "They have each other and they're welcome. But us loners ought to stick together."

"Heinrich's been a great comfort to me," Gia said, giving Victor a stern look that he interpreted as, *This is how dinner will be. Heinrich stays. Put up with him or piss off.*

"We need another menu," Victor sighed, looking around for the waiter.

"No, no, not for me," said Heinrich. "I never eat from the menu. I have very specific dietary demands."

"Yes, I saw you eating something the other night," said Victor. "What was that?"

"Kalbshirn," said Heinrich. "Calf's brain."

"Oh Heinrich," Gia groaned, the ends of her mouth curling upward in a twisted smile.

"They had calf brains in the kitchen?" said Victor.

Prince of Nightmares

"No, but they're very accommodating," said Heinrich. "I emailed ahead with the recipe and they made sure to get enough in stock to feed me throughout the week, no extra charge. In fact, I'm sure they brought in more than I require, if you want to try it."

"You're serious?"

"Oh yes. It's very good, you know. A delicacy in Germany. They tend to deep-fry it and put it in sandwiches, but this way's a little healthier, a little more refined. It's lightly poached and sautéed with mushrooms, very good. It assists with the dreams, too."

"In what way?"

"In *every* way."

Victor tapped a finger against the table and looked from Heinrich to the girl. Both their eyes were on him. "I've been having difficulty, just lately, telling the dreams from reality," he admitted.

"Oh it will definitely help with that," Heinrich said, as though the problem was well known to him. "Most certainly."

Victor nodded. "All right. I'll give it a try."

Gia laughed. "Really?"

"That's right. You in?"

She didn't hesitate. "Absolutely."

The waiter approached. "Ready to order?"

"Three for the brains, Dennis," said Victor. "And don't spare the horses. Seems we've all brought our appetites tonight."

14

Dinner was surprisingly civil. Victor never quite warmed to Heinrich, but it was easy enough to find common ground when the conversation was focused on the Ballador.

"I was standing in a lake of black," Heinrich said over coffee and brandy. "It was raining heavily and the water was slowly rising above my knees. There was no land in sight, only dark sky and dark waters, but in the distance I could see pale forms lifting themselves out of the water. They looked not unlike jellyfish, with large, cauliflower-shaped heads and long, awkwardly-angled tendrils, stiff enough to walk on. And they came striding towards me through the waves."

He swallowed hard, briefly back in the moment. "I turned and ran, but the waters kept rising, thickening like soup, so of course I got nowhere. I think that was the most terrifying—the point when you're trying to escape from an impossible menace as it bears down upon you. Out there," he said as he waved his hand at the window, meaning the entire outside world. "That would be the point at which the nightmare would end, the dreamer startled awake by fright. Not here, of course. Here, the nightmare continues."

"What did they do?" Gia asked, morbidly fascinated.

Heinrich ran his fingers along his neck, as though caressing an old wound. "They had razors on the ends of their limbs. When I think about it, I can still recall how they felt as they slid down my throat." His eyes flickered to Victor. "That was my first time. And very standard. Monsters, violation, pain, the loss of willpower. What I've learned is

Prince of Nightmares

that it needn't be that way. With the right skills, understanding and practice, one can take control of the nightmare and shape it to whatever one desires."

"That's why you eat brains!" Gia exclaimed.

Heinrich nodded. "It certainly helps."

Victor shifted a little uncomfortably in his chair and cleared his throat. "You're saying that you can bend the dreams to your will?"

"I'm saying anyone can with the right attitude."

"And once you've mastered it, you can . . . recreate memories? Places you've been, things you've done, people you've known?"

Heinrich made a face illustrating just how pedestrian he found the concept. "I can't see why you'd want to, but yes, I'm sure you could play with your past however you wished. It's like a big canvas really, once you've figured it out. The dreamer is only limited by his imagination."

Victor frowned. "But how is any of this possible?"

Heinrich shrugged. "Everyone has their own theories. Black magic, infrasound, the intersecting of psychic ley lines . . . even aliens."

Victor glanced over Heinrich's shoulder to the table where Paul and Karen had been sitting. It was empty now. "I spoke to a couple who seemed to think it was all the work of poltergeists. They were very sure of their history."

"Ah, yes," Heinrich grinned. "The so-called 'Residents.' The Crystal Mistress, Black Worm, Giant and their whole grotesque cavalcade."

"That's right."

"It's nonsense. A complete fantasy. It was all fabricated for the guide book."

"I don't know about that," Victor said. "The Drowned Maid sounded a lot like something I saw. And the guests I spoke to were convinced they'd seen them all except the Master of the . . . whatever."

"Oh, I'm quite sure people encounter the same

John McNee

mysterious figures," said Heinrich. "But anything you heard about their origins—young Mrs Minniver or whomever tragically strangled herself with her own underwear in 1876 and now haunts the pantry—is all a fiction. The company that now owns the Ballador also own a chain of haunted hotels across Europe. They employ copywriters to embellish the truth wherever they can get away with it. It's all a marketing ploy. Most people—like those you spoke to—just accept it because they're unwilling to scrape below the surface. They're the kind of people who come here looking for ghosts in the first place. They're not interested in the possibility of it being anything else."

Gia, who had been quiet for some considerable time, cleared her throat and, in a worried voice, asked, "What do you think it is, Heinrich?"

The man shrugged and smiled. "Oh, so many things. I agree with anyone who says it's more than the subconscious. There's unquestionably something invasive about it." He reached for his coffee cup and tilted it towards him, staring down into the black liquid, but not raising it to his lips. "When I was very young, growing up in Willhelmsburg, my great-grandmother liked to tell me that nightmares were the work of demonic creatures that crept into your bedroom while you were asleep and sat on your chest, pinning you to the bed. Frightening thing to tell a child, really. She called them *Alps* and the only way to protect yourself against them was to make sure every entrance into your room was stopped up tight before you went to sleep. And there was a charm she taught me.

"I lay me here to sleep. No nightmare shall plague me, until they swim all the waters that flow upon the earth and count all the stars that appear in the firmament. Thus help me God Father, Son, and Holy Ghost. Amen."

"You believe that?" Gia asked.

"I believe it's as likely as anything else," he answered. "What about you?"

Prince of Nightmares

Gia looked at Victor and for the briefest moment all he saw was the face of a confused and frightened little girl. There was something of significance in her eyes. Something she wanted desperately for him to understand. "I don't think they're nightmares at all," she said. "I think they're real. I think everything that happens to us in the dreams is real."

Heinrich laughed and slapped his palm down on the table. "If only that were the case!"

Gia smiled and laughed with him, the frightened girl hidden from sight once more. The change in her demeanour was so instantaneous Victor couldn't be sure he'd really seen what he thought.

"Well, this has all been rather wonderful," Heinrich said, taking a silver cigarette case from his pocket. "But I need a smoke. You don't smoke, do you Victor?"

"No."

"Wise man. Filthy habit. But we all have our vices." He grinned again as he rose from his chair. "I'll bid you both good night. We must meet again tomorrow and exchange what else we've seen."

Gia stood and kissed him on both cheeks.

Victor remained seated. "Good night, Heinrich."

The German gave a casual sort of salute, black cigarette already clutched between his fingers, and started out through the dining room toward the rear garden.

"Already knew who I was then, did you?" Victor said to Gia when they were both alone.

The girl's elbow was on the table, chin propped up in her hand, very relaxed. "Were you keeping it a secret?"

He shook his head. "I just didn't think you knew, that's all."

"Heinrich told me some. I found out a little more on the internet."

He winced. "Probably doesn't paint me in the most flattering light."

"Which part?"

"Any of it. All of it."

She narrowed her eyes, then glanced away from him, and he could tell she was thinking it over. "You're concerned about my behaviour."

"I'm concerned about a lot of things."

"But, in particular, you're worried that a woman like me, knowing the things about you that I know, would never behave towards you in the manner that I have. Not unless I had a motive."

"I never used to care about my reputation. Only lately." His mind's eye glanced upon a message scrawled on the mirror of a Sydney hotel bathroom.

Gia sighed. "Honestly? I don't care about your reputation. But I am interested in what you're doing here."

"And if I asked the same of you?"

She smiled and raised an eyebrow. "I could tell you the whole sorry story. But you might not think much of me by the end."

Victor raised his coffee cup in mock toast and nodded. "Similarly."

Dozens of midges flew in dizzying clouds beneath the patio lights. The creatures were a menace at this time of year. Heinrich found he always seemed to attract them for some reason. And they bit. Having lit a cigarette, he blew smoke at them, but they weren't dissuaded, so he flapped his arm through the swarm and stalked off into the garden, hoping they'd remain in the light.

His journey took him into the shadows beyond the hedges, within sight of the Ballador's much-admired towering oak tree. He looked back at the hotel, staring up at the bedroom windows on the first and second floors. His eyes lingered on the first, knowing they were the windows to Gia's suite. They were dark now, but he wondered how long it would be before they were illuminated and who might be with her at the time.

Prince of Nightmares

He'd been surprised by Gia at dinner. Though he'd personally found Teversham a little unremarkable—certainly a disappointment, given his reputation—she'd seemed positively captivated. Even though Heinrich had been doing most of the talking, Gia's eyes had hardly strayed from the antipodean widower for more than a minute. If it was his money that had caught her attention, well . . . he could appreciate that. But he didn't believe she was a gold digger, so her behaviour had rather thrown him.

Not that it was a competition, not at all. His feelings shouldn't have been hurt. Given his age and proclivities, Heinrich hardly expected beautiful young women to wilt in his presence, but to pass him over for a man as dour as Victor Teversham was still a little insulting. Perhaps he'd failed to pick up on some rather obvious quality in the man. He'd have to ask Gia what he was missing, if he ever got the chance. Certainly, he knew he was missing something.

Casting the pair from his mind and turning away from the hotel, he spotted a figure a few yards away. In the gloom, he could make out little more than a dark outline, but he could see enough to know it was a woman, standing beneath the oak tree. She was facing him.

Heinrich, not wanting to appear unfriendly, raised his hand and gave a little wave.

The woman remained perfectly motionless, giving no response.

He thought perhaps it was too dark for her to see him clearly, so waved again and called out, "Good evening!"

At this, the woman turned slowly and walked behind the tree. In profile, Heinrich was able to see she had short hair, cut in a bob, and wore a long overcoat. But then she was gone.

He squinted at the spot where she had stood moments before, his mind racing through the brief catalogue of women staying or employed at the hotel, trying to think of one who might fit her silhouette.

When he couldn't think of one, he took a last drag on the

cigarette, flicked it into the bushes, and followed her to the other side of the tree.

"He's a what?" said Victor.

"A dominator," Gia replied. "Male dominatrix. You know. Don't pretend you don't."

"So women *pay* him to . . . "

"And men." Gia nodded. "I don't think he discriminates."

"As though I needed another reason to dislike him."

She pouted. "Don't be like that. I like him. And he was perfectly pleasant to you given all the terrible things he's heard about you."

"After a fashion, yes. You shouldn't believe everything you read, you know."

"Tell me it your own way," she said. "I'm here. I've got nowhere to go. You could tell me your whole life story if you wanted."

"I wouldn't know where to start." He sighed. "And the abridged highlights probably wouldn't make me look any better."

"I'm not looking to judge. I've done a few things myself I'm not proud of. The only difference is that nothing I ever did made me rich. It's almost worse in its way. Wrong for the sake of it."

"No." Victor shook his head. "Let's not. I don't want to turn this into a shared confessional. I'd much rather we kept things light and just had a nice friendly chat."

She smiled. "All right, Victor. Shall we take this to the bar?"

He nodded and rose from his seat. "After you."

"Hello there?" Heinrich came around the oak tree on the right side, following in the footsteps of the woman. He came around the trunk expecting to find her leaning against it—he was quite sure she hadn't come round again—but there was no one there.

Prince of Nightmares

He popped his head around one side, then the other—feeling foolish as he did so—then ducked back to where he imagined she'd been standing and assumed the same position he'd imagined her to have assumed, leaning one shoulder against the tree and fishing in his jacket pocket for his cigarette case.

From his location he could see a small section of the grounds stretching towards the tree line and, beyond that, the mountains. Lighting another cigarette, he had to wonder where the woman had disappeared to. He was certain he'd seen her and *quite* certain she couldn't have walked away without him witnessing it. He considered it doubtful in the extreme that she had actually climbed the oak, but he turned his head upwards anyway just to be sure.

It was while he was staring up through the branches that he felt something snap at his foot. Startled, he jumped to the right and almost tripped, his foot staying where it was. Something had wound its way around his shoe and was pinching him. He tugged, kicked and finally pulled himself free, before bending down to get a closer look at what had grabbed him.

Squinting to make out details in the darkness, he saw the stem of a thick, black weed, heavy with thorns, curling upwards through the grass. He looked on, eyes widening, as the weed snaked its way up from the soil, bringing friends with it. They twisted and coiled, rising to the surface like a plague of black earthworms. Then, when they'd pulled themselves up sufficiently far, they bent their thorns towards Heinrich and reached out for him.

Heinrich didn't want or need to see any more. He straightened up and began staggering back towards the hotel, his eyes still on the patch of ground under the tree. When he was too far away to see the weeds any more, he turned his head towards the building . . . and froze in his tracks.

The cigarette tumbled from his gasping pink mouth.

There were some new guests in the lounge area. A pair of young couples laughing together over a bottle of wine at a corner table. Dennis, now serving drinks at the bar, said they were standard tourists with rooms in the extension and no knowledge, or interest, in the Ballador's more unique features. Gia, perched on the stool next to Victor, asked where the newcomers were from, but Victor didn't hear the reply.

He was watching one of the girls. The brunette. He was thinking of how much she reminded him of Josie when she was young. The long dark hair. The slender, almost fragile arms. The way she sat, the way she held her wine glass, the way she laughed.

When the girl threw her head back, mouth open in a broad smile, Victor caught sight of a bullet hole in her temple, leaking a thin stream of blood down her cheek.

"Victor?"

He jumped at the touch of Gia's hand on his arm. "Sorry. I'm sorry."

"Are you all right?" Her brow was creased in concern.

"I'll be fine." He picked up his glass and raised it to his lips. "Sorry. It's . . . nothing to worry about. I just . . . lately, I've been having these little . . . momentary hallucinations. You been getting anything like that?"

She shook her head. The concern hadn't lifted from her face.

Victor smirked. "Must just be me then."

"Are you tired?"

"No more than . . . " The words died on his tongue. He was looking into the mirror on the rear wall of the bar, staring past his reflection, into the lobby behind him and the woman who stood there. Blonde, mid-forties, wide-eyed, she stared straight back.

He knew the face. It took him a moment, but he got there. He remembered her covered in blood, reaching an arm up towards him, clinging desperately to a wall of shattered glass.

"It's not possible." He spun about and jumped up off the stool.

"Victor?" Gia said, though again he didn't hear it.

His eyes were on the woman, who stared back, appearing just as shocked and confused as him. He started across the lounge towards her, but she turned and fled, darting up the main stairs and out of sight. Victor pressed on, into the lobby, finding Mrs Dempsey behind the desk.

"Who was that?" he demanded.

"I'm sorry?"

"The woman who just ran up the stairs. The blonde."

"Oh. Um . . . Mrs Forrester? She's a guest."

"A guest?"

Mrs Demspey nodded in a worried way. "That's right. Haven't you met?"

"Victor!" Gia had chased him from the bar. Her hands were on his arm, pulling him around. "What is it? What's wrong?"

"It's . . . I don't . . . " He pulled away from her, hands over his face. "Just . . . just give me a minute." He was trying to figure it out. Trying to understand how a woman he'd only ever seen in a nightmare could be a fellow guest in the hotel. He was thinking back over the past few days, trying to remember if maybe he'd spotted her somewhere else, if they'd passed each other in the hall, the restaurant, the car park.

No. The crystal cliff. That had been their first and only encounter. He'd recognised the shock on her face as matching—perhaps eclipsing—his own. And why wouldn't it? From her perspective, presuming they'd both shared the same dream—and that, he'd quickly realised, was what this meant—he was the sadistic spectre who had kicked her to a screaming death. She'd had good reason to run. Same thing went for . . .

Victor remembered the look on Paul's face at dinner. That unexpected, unwarranted glare of hatred, fear, revulsion, and contempt. Or not so unwarranted, when you took into account the whole business with the hot tar.

When he thought back on the dream, Victor had taken Paul and Karen for ciphers, dredged up from his subconscious and given form by the unseen forces of the Ballador. Clearly, he'd given those 'unseen forces' too little credit. This felt like something much more extraordinary and much more calculated.

And there was something else. "What room is Heinrich in?" he asked Gia.

"Heinrich? He's above me, but . . . he won't be there, he's . . . "

"Show me," said Victor. "It's important. Show me the room."

There was a commonality to the reviews of some of the Ballador's most satisfied customers. When they wrote of the experience, in trying to summarise what they had seen, heard, and felt in a way that was both comprehensible and palatable to potential visitors, a great many focused on the theme of 'nostalgia.'

More specifically, it was the nostalgia of terror.

It was a common complaint among those who liked to be scared that they rarely ever were any more. When they spoke of wanting to experience something that would truly frighten them again, they meant in the way that they had been frightened as children, when every sound and shadow in a darkened room promised the approach of unspeakable abominations.

Growing up, imagination gave way to cynicism. Ignorance was traded in for world-weariness. Fears remained, but they were the dull, suburban fears of illness, destitution, and death. The visceral terror of the unknown—of unseen things lurking under the bed or creeping out of the cupboard—became a fuzzy memory. Until a privileged few discovered the Ballador, attempts to rediscover such incapacitating terrors had proved disappointing at best. All the horrors of cinema, literature, news media, and the modern waking world couldn't compare with the monsters of childhood for inspiring sheer, unrelenting dread.

It was that same, all-encompassing fear that Heinrich felt now, coursing through his veins, as he stood in the garden, knowing he was awake and watching as an unfathomable creature dragged itself up from the earth.

Its shoulders were first to break through, wide and thick like a bull's. To Heinrich it appeared at first like a big, grey boulder shooting up through the soil, but then came the arms, scattering clumps of grass and dirt as they reached up for the sky, then slapped back down. The hands—large, calloused, and five-fingered—dug in as grey muscles tensed, pushing down as the beast's back arched, sucking its twisted flesh body out of the ground. It resembled a fat clump of hair pulled from a drain—a long, serpent-like tail of knotted black fibres, spiralling around each other, finishing in a neat, sharp point. The soil around and beneath undulated with the twitching of more black weeds and Heinrich began to see points at which they still clung to the creature's arms and body.

The beast was fruit of the weed. Heinrich recognised this in the moment before the shoulders jerked and tugged the heavy head from the earth like a ripe turnip. The face was a deformed, babyish caricature of his own, with bulging eyes like a pair of white goldfish bowls in a mask of wet, black clay. Its lipstick-painted lips peeled open to reveal a mouth of smiling daggers.

"Heinrich," it said.

John McNee

Victor stood in the second floor hallway. He'd never been up here before, but he knew it from the dream. The door at the far end led to the room of Mrs Forrester, where he'd stood at the top of the glass cliff. The room across from it belonged to Paul and Karen—the Swarm, the flesh-ripping factory.

The door at which he now stood was the same one he hadn't dared cross in the dream. The room of metal hooks, mutilated bodies, and in the corner, a man of molten black, with phosphorescent eyes.

Heinrich.

"He was telling the truth," Victor said. "All that stuff about will. He can turn the trick. I saw it for myself, but I didn't understand what I was seeing. I took him for one of *them*. Another Resident."

"Are you so certain he's not?" Gia stood at the top of the stairs, arms folded across her chest. "Are you so certain *you're* not?" She asked it almost petulantly.

"What?"

"Floating through other people's nightmares, Victor? That goes beyond what even Heinrich was talking about. It's not fucking possible." There was an attitude to her voice, a kind of aggression. He couldn't discern where it was coming from. Confusion? Incredulity? Jealousy?

Fear. It all came back to fear.

"None of this should be possible, Gia. Not a bit of it." His own voice was getting louder now.

"What did you do in their dreams?" She took a step towards him. "What did you do to them that they're all so frightened of you now?"

He'd left that part out of the story. A little on-the-hoof self-editing. "I . . . don't remember."

She laughed—a single, sarcastic syllable. "And do you remember forcing your way into anyone else's dreams? Or have you forgotten all about that as well?"

"What are you . . . " He took a step towards her and went down, his foot plunging through the carpet and into icy liquid, like he'd stumbled through a crack in a frozen lake.

"Victor!" Gia caught his arms as he fell and he dragged her down, the two of them crumpling into an awkward heap on the floor.

Gasping from the shock, he rolled onto his side and pulled his foot free, expecting to splash water up the wall and prepared to find a jagged black hole in the carpet.

There was no hole. No water. His leg was perfectly dry, though the chilling sensation clung to his skin.

"What was that?" Gia asked, pulling herself back onto her feet, careful to adjust her dress. "Are you all right?"

Victor, still on his back, was a little breathless. "Fine."

"Another hallucination?" She helped him up.

"Not that," he said. "I shouldn't have called them that. I just . . . I think I'm a little more tired than I realised."

She nodded sympathetically, took his arm and led him down the stairs. He didn't need her support, not really. Yet it was nice to feel her so close, and he was loathe to push her away, even if letting her near made him seem like a helpless invalid.

They descended in silence. She led him to the door of his suite, rubbed her hand along his arm in a comforting way. "Get some rest," she said.

He nodded, found his key, and put it in the lock while she wandered back across the landing to her own suite.

His door opened into a wall of black. Victor held his ground, staring into the room, waiting for his eyes to adjust. Waiting for the shadows to take shape. Nothing. The void remained a formless abyss that light seemed fearful to penetrate. Yet he knew it wasn't empty. Somewhere in the darkness, something waited for him.

"Of course . . . " He flinched at Gia's voice, surprised she was still in the hall. "You're welcome to join me for another drink."

He turned slowly around to see her standing at the open door to the Library Suite, leaning against the wall, hands behind her back, chest puffed out. The room beyond glowed with warm golden light.

"I've got some wine," she said. "If you're not quite up to facing the dreams again. I know I'm not."

Victor glanced back into his own room. The darkness churned. He was scared of venturing inside. Afraid he'd be swallowed alive. "Maybe . . . not just yet."

She crossed the distance between them, moving with a dancer's grace. She bowed her head, eyes on the floor in a calculated display of vulnerability. "I don't want you to think of me poorly. I'm no seductress, but . . . " Her hand found its way to his wrist. She looked up at him with eyes that shone. "It's not easy, enduring the dreams each night alone. No one to talk to. No one to . . . share your bed."

In spite of everything, this took him by surprise. He scowled and pulled his hand away from her. "How old are you?"

She rolled her eyes and drew closer to him, her leg brushing against his. "Is that so important to you?"

"I could be your grandfather."

Her hand crept up his arm, reaching his shoulder. "But you're *not* my grandfather. Besides, you don't look *so* old . . . "

The line pricked at his vanity. He felt a smile creep up the side of his face, almost allowing himself to give in to the girl's advances, before realising how ridiculous it was. How like a *fantasy*.

Which raised other concerns.

"I . . . I'm flattered," he said.

She leaned closer, backing him up against the wall. "You don't find me attractive?"

"That's not the issue," he replied, wanting to check the door to his room for creeping tentacles, but afraid to look away from her, lest her face should suddenly dissolve into a black crater.

Prince of Nightmares

"Then what is the issue?"

I don't think you're real. "It's nothing. Really."

She grinned as she lit upon his worry. "I think I know." Her hand moved up the back of his neck, running fingers through his sparse grey hair. Her breath was warm on his mouth and carried the scent of coffee—bitter and sweet. "You think you're dreaming."

His eyes scanned her face for a trace of the visions from his nightmares, but the beautiful mask was flawless. She cocked her head a little to the left, the hair falling out of her face. He half-expected to see a leaking bullet wound in her temple, but there was none.

"Kiss me," she said, her eyes already half-closed. "Then tell me you're dreaming."

He did so, against his better judgement, and discovered there was nothing otherworldly about it. Her lips were soft, warm and quite real.

16

It was raining hard along the Ayrshire coast. Harry was relieved to see lights were on in the little bungalow and jogged up the path to the door, the collar of his jacket tugged up over his head. He rang the doorbell and spent the minute before it was answered wiping rainwater from his face and condensation from his glasses.

The woman who opened the door appeared very small, very old, and well used to being both. Her mouth formed a welcoming smile that didn't quite reach her eyes, which squinted over the rim of a pair of reading glasses. "Yes?"

Raising his voice over the noisy patter of the rain, Harry did his best to explain who he was and who he worked for.

The names clearly meant nothing to her. But at the mention of Fergus McLoughty her eyebrow crept up.

Harry shrugged apologetically. "I am aware of the hour."

Evelyn Burgess stared at him for several long, silent seconds. "Well, you'd better come in if you're coming," she said.

She insisted on making tea. Harry waited in the living room, surrounded by shelves of books, ornaments, and curiosities. She had an old-fashioned three-bar electric fire, which bathed the room in an unnatural orange haze. He was warming himself in front of it, casting a long shadow on the rug, when she returned.

"Was it Gordon Gallan who sent you to me?" she asked, placing a tray down on the coffee table.

"Uh, yes," said Harry. "Directed, rather than sent. I would have called ahead, but there was no number."

She waved a brittle hand. "I don't have a phone. No television, no internet, no family, no friends. I'd never have any visitors at all if it weren't for Gordon Gallan sending me oddballs. No offence." She held out a cup of tea.

He smiled as he accepted it. "None taken. Turning up on your doorstep in the night, in the pouring rain . . . I'd call that pretty odd myself."

She took a seat in a well-cushioned armchair and directed him to the ancient sofa opposite. "You're here about Peter, are you?"

He frowned. "Peter?"

"PTR." She smiled. "Projected Telekinetic Reconfiguration. Or *Peter*, for short. It's why everyone comes here. Haven't written a word about it in fifty years, but there always seems to be another generation of the Third Eye Brigade eager to seek me out."

Harry laughed bemusedly. "Uh, no. I, uh . . . I never even heard of that. It sounds . . . " He didn't want to say how it sounded. "It really sounds like something."

The old woman stared at him hard for a few moments, eyes locked on his. "Put the cup down," she said.

"Sorry?"

"Put it down."

He did as he was asked, setting the tea cup and saucer on the table in front of him. He wondered if he'd offended her and immediately began drafting an apology in his head. What a waste it would be, to have come all this way for nothing. "Miss Burgess, I . . . "

"Quiet," she said. "Look at me. Look at my eyes."

Shit, he thought. *The old broad's going to try to hypnotise me.* Still, he went with it, returning her gaze and inwardly cringing from the fear she might at any moment produce a pocket watch and begin counting backwards from a hundred. There was a clarity to her eyes. They sparkled like they were new.

"Mm hmm," she mumbled, breaking the stare after less

than a minute, and raising her own cup to her lips. "Now I want you to do one other thing."

"What's that?"

"Turn your head to the right. Look at the wall."

Confused, he did as commanded and saw something he hadn't noticed before. There was a hole in the wall—gaping and ugly, roughly six inches in diameter, as though a cannon shell had punched through the brick. A thin trail of grey slime oozed down the wallpaper and Harry could see movement within—something twisting and turning in the darkness—like he was peering down one end of a long, black tunnel. He turned his head slightly, angling his ear towards it as he noticed a sound, like the hiss of steam, and felt a rush of cold air on his face.

He leaned forward, narrowing his eyes, and then jerked back as the hole exploded a fountain of snakes.

"Jesus Christ!" He leaped out of his chair, stumbling over his feet, eyes on the wall, watching scores of skinny black serpents flowering out into the room, some clinging to the wall like their scales had been painted with wet glue, others dropping to the floor, landing with sickening wet slaps and slithering out towards him. Harry collided with a bookcase and screamed.

"Oh relax," Evelyn chided. Her tea cup was up at her lips.

Harry saw snakes crowding upon her, moving like black shadows across the carpet. Others pressed on towards him, vicious little heads raised in anger, mouths open, fangs ready. "Get out!" He cried. "We have to get out!"

"Harry."

"What?"

"Harry!"

He turned to face her, eyes wide behind his glasses.

She shook her head. "There's nothing there."

"What?" He turned back. The snakes—all of them—had vanished. There was no hole in the wall, no slime, no tunnel into oblivion . . . nothing. "What?" He looked again at the old woman. "What was that? What the hell just happened?"

Evelyn shrugged. "Just a little show. Sit yourself back down."

Harry was out of breath, his heart racing, back still up against the bookcase. He didn't quite feel ready to return to his seat on the sofa that a moment ago he'd seen crawling with snakes. "You . . . you hypnotised me."

"No."

"Then . . . then what? Christ, what could even . . . ?"

"*That* was PTR. Neither hypnotism nor hallucination, difficult to replicate under laboratory conditions and close to impossible to describe to someone who hasn't seen it for themselves."

"You . . . you suggested images," Harry said. "There was something you said . . . "

Evelyn shook her head. "I didn't tell you to see snakes. I asked you to look at the wall."

"You saw snakes?"

She smiled. "I saw snakes. You saw snakes. And so there were snakes. It's all in the eyes."

"They weren't real."

"Real enough. If they'd bit you, you'd have bled."

"That's impossible."

She cringed. "Please don't use that word. It's insulting as well as boring."

Harry staggered back to the sofa and practically fell into it. He picked up his tea, wishing it was something stronger. "How did you do that?"

She rolled her eyes. "Now there's a question. I wasted almost half my life trying to figure out how I'm able to do the things I can do. It's an innate ability, you see. I don't remember ever not being able to . . . well . . . "

"Muster snakes out of thin air?"

"Not just snakes. Cats, dogs, fire, water, gold, silver. It only lasts as long as I can hold the thought, but for those few moments . . . it's all quite real. Quite solid."

"It's not possible."

"You don't know what's possible," she snapped. "Nobody does! As a species, we're not even *capable*. You appreciate the nature of reality the same way a gnat appreciates jazz."

Harry raised an eyebrow. "If you say so."

She sighed. "I wrote books about this. Me and others. They didn't sell. It's like I said, it's a hard thing to communicate to someone who isn't in the room. Fergus McLoughty was one of the few who read one and seemed to understand. Or at least interested to learn."

"McLoughty did?"

She nodded. "There was a lot more serious interest in psychic phenomena back in the sixties. Now it's all a joke—a circus for charlatans and idiots. Back then, it was different. Back then, there were people who hoped we were on the brink of a new world, the first of an evolved generation. It all seems childishly optimistic now."

"And McLoughty?"

"He was a cripple who desperately wanted to walk again. With all the established medical routes closed to him, he searched for other ways. Telekinesis, astral projection . . . Eventually he found me. And with me, he walked."

Harry shook his head. He touched a hand to his forehead and found it dappled with sweat. "Because you imagined him walking?"

"I *perceived* it. You see, it's perception and reality. We consider them two different concepts—one a tool enabling us to qualify the other, when really they impact one upon the other in ways we can't even comprehend. That's the least of it. The truth is the space between them is so paper thin they're practically one and the same."

"You might have to slow down," said Harry. "Just back it up a second."

"I have a book." Evelyn rose from her chair and shuffled across to one of the bookcases. She kept on with the story as she rifled through the shelves. "He wanted to walk. I perceived him walking. And so he walked. But only when I was in the room. Only when I was there to perceive it. And so he became obsessed with learning how to do it for himself."

"You taught him how? You can do that?"

She sighed. "No. But I tried. I had friends at the time with similar skills. With McLoughty's money and resources we were able to find others. He gave us use of one of his country houses and we turned it into a sort of experimental compound."

"The Ballador."

She tensed and turned her head slowly around to face him. "How do you know that?"

Harry gave a little smile, pleased with himself for finally managing to shock her, even if it was only in a small way. "It's why I'm here."

The lines on her brow deepened. She was clearly concerned, but turned back to the books, busying herself with them for the moment. "The hope was that living together, far away from the distractions of the outside world, and filling our days with psychic exercises, we might reach, if not a breakthrough, then at least a progression."

"Psychic exercises?"

"It's simpler than it sounds. We'd gather in groups in the library, arrange ourselves to form what's called a 'psychic chain' and then . . . there were a few different things we could try, variations on the snake trick. Visualisation was the main one, all of us focusing our minds to create something out of thin air, sharing its inception. Physical manipulation, astral projection, imprinting. The challenge there is to impose your own consciousness on another. That was interesting. We had real success with insects and rodents, but swapping out one person's mind for another's seemed beyond us."

"It sounds like something from a comic book."

"We didn't think so at the time. It felt like we were pushing forward into the next stage of human evolution, like we were on the cusp of creating a better world. We believed the potential to be dormant in the mind of every man and woman. And we thought with enough time, enough energy and focus, we might find the key to unlock it in everyone."

"You still believe that?"

She bowed her head. "Less so, now. I think it takes a very particular type of person. At least we gave it a good shot. Almost five years. No one can say we gave up easily." She lifted a battered hardback from the shelf. "Here we are."

"How many of you were living at the Ballador?"

Evelyn shrugged as she came back to her chair. "Maybe a dozen, plus Fergus. I have a picture." She opened the book at the back page, where an envelope of black and white photographs had been filed. "One of these."

Harry leaned forward. "Tell me about the nightmares."

She flinched, jerking back in her chair and nearly dropping the book. Her hand moved instinctively to her heart. "I'd rather not discuss that."

"But you know what I'm talking about," Harry said, pressing the point. "You know, don't you?"

Her eyes darted around the room. "We were pioneers in a new field of science, dealing with forces that, to this day, remain beyond the comprehension of even the most brilliant minds. We couldn't know every variable, every possible outcome. You have to understand . . . " Finally her eyes found his, her voice wavering. "It was inevitable that there would be side effects."

"What do you mean?"

"No." She shook her head emphatically, eyes back on the book, the envelope, rifling through it for the photo she wanted. "No, I don't . . . I don't want to talk about that."

"Miss Burgess . . . "

"No." She waved her hand dismissively. "It's in the past, it's in the past." She sounded on the verge of tears and Harry felt unable to push on, but then she grinned. "Here it is."

She held out the photograph and, not wanting to upset her further, Harry accepted it. He turned it toward the light from the fire and saw Ballador House as it stood in 1966, with a row of smiling young hippies lined up in front of it, squinting in the sunshine. In their midst stood an older gentleman, with oiled blond hair and a tweed suit.

"That's Fergus McLoughty," Evelyn said, pointing with a quivering finger. "He's standing, you see? You see? He's standing because I'm there with him, on the left. You see?"

The woman on McLoughty's left was small like Evelyn, and thin, like Evelyn, but young, perhaps not even 30, with braided hair and dangling earrings, barefoot in blue jeans and a knitted wool jumper. She grinned with a cigarette clamped between her teeth. "I see," Harry said, trying to be polite, trying to humour her, even though all he really wanted to do was bombard her with questions about the nightmares. She had the answers. She could solve every mystery rattling around his head if she were only willing to talk. "Really, it's a nice picture. Very . . . "

He let the sentence trail off as his eyes fell upon another face in the photograph—a woman near the end of the line on the right side. A young woman with long dark hair, fair skin and belly so swollen even the maternity dress seemed to be struggling to contain it. Harry bent his head forward, squinting to see her features in the gloom. Even in the fire's half-light, the resemblance was unmistakable.

"Who's she?" he asked, raising the picture and pointing to the woman.

Evelyn narrowed her eyes, and then smiled broadly. "Ah, yes. Agnes Morrison. Such a sweetheart, she really was, and so *talented*."

"She's pregnant."

"Well, yes," said Evelyn. "She wasn't when she arrived. But, communal living, a bunch of single young men and women rooming together for months at a time. You do your best to prevent that sort of thing, but, well . . . it's human nature, isn't it? All worked out in the end. I think she married the young lad involved. Ah, but I haven't thought about her in years! You know it really was quite the episode when the time finally came. Ended up, she gave birth right on the floor of the library."

Harry could feel the legs of invisible spiders creeping their way up his spine. "That so?"

"Oh, yes." Evelyn grinned. "Gosh, I remember it so clearly. It was a little baby girl she had. Named her Josephine."

17

It was a curious thing, Victor thought to himself. She hadn't a spoken a word of French the whole day. Not on the mountaintop, nor on the long journey down, in the restaurant, at the bar, or in the hall. Only in bed did her mother tongue reassert itself.

It made him wonder how honest she'd been with him over the course of their few hours together. Perhaps it had all been an act. She was a performer, after all, so she had to be capable. When he considered it, it made a little sense. Her animated chatter on the trail, switching gears over dinner, rapidly cycling through masks of confidence, shyness and seduction—all acts, all keeping him off balance while keeping her guard up. Only in her room—in her *bed*—did she show any sign of her true self.

She was afraid.

That much was to be expected. He'd seen flickers of it throughout the evening. Every guest in the hotel liked to be scared. It was the whole appeal. Only with Gia, there was a significant qualifier. To her, fear was erotic. It was an aphrodisiac.

And, as near as he could tell, she found Victor *terrifying*.

She lay naked and vulnerable beneath him, shivering like an ignorant virgin, flinching at the touch of his fingers as they traced the contours of her body, muttering prayers and exclamations in French.

For Victor, all thoughts of propriety and immorality evaporated at the touch of her kiss. Gia may have been the one who pulled him across the threshold into her suite, but once inside he was fully committed to the task, his body invigorated by lust.

Before this night, he'd doubted he was still capable of sex. He was what the world perceived him to be—a frail, impotent old man.

Yet, if he had to gauge his performance, he might even call it good. He might call it *exemplary*. What strength he had. What stamina. At almost eighty years old he felt young, strong, vital. The house, he knew, had to be part of it, but how?

He considered this question some time afterwards, lying alone in bed as Gia showered in the en suite. Such mysteries to consider. Pieces of the puzzle fluttered about in his head, but he lacked the capacity for analysis. His brain was a post-coital soup, not quite up to the task. He wanted to sleep, but was apprehensive of what that might bring.

So he dragged himself out from under the sheets and took a solitary tour of the suite, more than a little curious to see the rooms which, at one time, had been reserved for him. And though he honestly didn't care in which room he slept, he had to admit he found it much more to his taste than the Honeymoon Suite.

The rooms, which in the Ballador's former life had formed the library, still retained many of its original and unique features, down to the hand-carved bookcase which took up most of the sitting room's western wall. Victor browsed through a couple of shelves, but didn't find anything very interesting. Volumes of encyclopaedias, digests, and hardback manuals filled the shelves, but it seemed they were there to fill space more than anything else.

He wandered over to the window—enjoying the feel of the plush rug under his bare feet—and peered out into the night. The view couldn't compete with his own of the loch, but there were a few items of interest still just visible in the darkness—the garden, hedgerows, oak tree. His eye caught the form of a figure. He squinted, trying to make it out, quickly recognising it was a woman. One of the new guests, it looked like. The one with the dark hair. Except . . .

"Ouch!"

He jerked as he felt a sharp pain in the sole of his foot and stumbled back. It felt like the snapping teeth of an insect. He glanced down, expecting to see blood, but there was none. What he did see was a small mound in the rug, like a rodent was camouflaged beneath the fibres.

From the bathroom he heard the sound of a tap being turned. The roar of the shower faded to a slow, echoing drip. "Gia?" he called. There was no answer, only the drip from the shower and a soft hum in his ears, like the angry buzzing of a fly.

The mound moved, heading away from him towards the edge of the rug. He kept his eyes on it, prepared to see a black-haired mouse go scurrying across the room. What emerged from the rug's edge was a mound in the hardwood floor, like a blister in the varnish. It kept on, gliding with ease to reach the wall, at which point it became a bulge in the skirting board, then a bubble in the wallpaper, rising to eye level and quickly joined by friends. As Victor watched, the wall began to ripple, bubbling like boiling liquid. An unnatural, impossible display.

"Gia!"

He ran back into the bedroom and found the rippling replicated in every surface. There was tension in every material, whether cotton, wood, brick, or steel. Small spears of fabric rose from the bed and carpet, as though fingers pressed up from beneath. The glass in the window and dressing table mirror contorted beyond physics to glove slender hands that reached into the room from unknown depths.

"Gia!"

He threw open the door to the bathroom and ventured inside, stepping through blinding clouds of white steam to reach the bathtub. The curtain was drawn. He tugged it back in the same moment every surface exploded, plunging him into darkness.

The buzz in his ears slowed and lowered in pitch to become a voice. A repeated phrase.

"*This is the room. Make ready. This is the room. Make ready. This is the room. Make ready. This is the room. Make ready. This is the room. Make ready. This is the room. Make ready . . .*"

Hands of tile and porcelain grabbed at his limbs, dragged him down, sucked him into a cold embrace. "No," he screamed. "Nooooo!"

"Victor! Calm down! Victor! It's okay! You're all right!"

Gia was on top of him, pinning him to the bed as he struggled beneath her, desperate to escape, fighting to survive. "Let me go," he cried. "Let me . . . I . . . " The thrashing eased, his voice lowered. "What? What happened?"

She laughed. "What do think? You were dreaming."

He blinked, the world slowly coming back into focus. He was out of breath and acutely aware of her naked body pressing down upon him. He shook his head. "No," he said. "There's no way. That wasn't a dream. That was real . . . "

She laughed again, kissed him on the cheek and rolled off. Her hair was wet. Moisture glistened on her skin. She picked her towel up from the floor, then rounded the bed and gathered up the sheets he'd thrown away. "I got out of the shower and you were going crazy," she said. "I thought you were going to tear the place apart."

He shook his head disbelievingly. "I can't tell what's real and what's not. It . . . didn't seem like a dream." He looked about the room, searching for some movement in the walls, in the window, the furniture. "Not like the others. Something new."

She threw the sheets over him, sat down at the foot of the bed and began to dry her hair. "You called my name in your sleep," she said. "It was very flattering."

18

"I'm afraid I really don't know what to tell you," said Mrs Dempsey, somehow managing to keep her tone civil though every fibre in her being longed to simply slam the phone down and be done with the conversation.

"Can you please just try again?" Harry insisted. "Please. I'm not asking a lot here."

"I don't know what good it would do," Mrs Dempsey said. "I've tried ringing the suite several times. Either Mr Teversham isn't there or he doesn't want to answer, which is entirely his right."

"Not there? It's after midnight. Where the hell would he be?"

"I'm sure I don't know. That's entirely his affair."

"You're saying you don't take the slightest responsibility for what happens to your guests? You don't care that he could be in serious danger?"

"I last saw Mr Teversham around an hour ago. He seemed in rude health. So no, I'm not concerned. Unless you'd care to elaborate on what you mean by 'serious danger'?"

There was silence on the line for a moment. "It's . . . complicated."

"I'm sure it is. And when I next see him I will be sure to let him know that you called."

"Send someone up to the room. Do me that much. Take a key, hammer a few times on the door, and if he doesn't answer—"

John McNee

"I do have other guests, you know. I don't intend to go waking them all just to—"

"But it's an *emergency!*"

"Is it?"

Another pause. "It *could* be! I mean . . . For all you know!"

"Have a good evening, sir."

"No! No! Do not hang up," Harry cried out on the other end of the line.

She never heard him.

Heinrich couldn't feel his legs.

When the creature spoke his name, he turned and fled, taking off into the woods, his feet moving faster than he'd thought possible. The beast pursued him, propelling itself forward with its arms, dragging its tail behind like a fat slug. It moved as quickly as he did, never more than a few yards behind for the first mile or so.

But Heinrich kept running, fortified by fear, his system overwhelmed by the energy of terror. He tore through trees, up rocky terrain, across a small stream, down into a gulley, hurtling left and scrambling to the right, his mouth wide open to suck down oxygen, eyes fixed on the ground ahead, desperate not to trip, head facing the front and never daring to look back.

He ran for hours. He ran until his legs ached and kept on, until they burned, until they screamed, until they died and went numb. He kept on running.

When at last he sprinted down a slope and broke through the trees, emerging onto a shore of black pebbles, he was forced to stop, look around, and get his bearings.

He stood facing the loch, having lost his way in the woods and practically doubled back on himself. Looking along the shore, he saw the silhouette of the Ballador, only a short distance away.

The beast was nowhere in sight.

Prince of Nightmares

"Mr Stritzel?" Mrs Dempsey was behind the desk to see him as he strode in through the front door. He looked a mess—suit caked in mud and grime, hands and face marked where branches had slashed him, skin dappled with a greasy mix of sweat, dirt, and blood.

Still breathless, clearly exhausted, he approached the desk and nodded by way of greeting. "Good evening. Would you please be so kind as to call me a taxicab?"

She frowned. "Mr Stritzel, are you quite all right?"

"Yes, yes, fine," he said a little irritably. "Would you please call me a taxicab? I wish to check out immediately."

"Check out? Is there something wrong with your room?"

"No. Well, yes, probably. But no, I . . . I just want to leave. Now. I want to leave."

"If you're dissatisfied with the room, we have others. I can offer you a bed in the extension if you'd rather—"

"No!" He slammed his palm down on the desk, leaving a bloody print behind. "I want a taxicab! I demand a taxicab!"

"Mr Stritzel, *please*," Mrs Dempsey said. "I have other guests. I don't wish them disturbed."

Heinrich stared down into his quivering hands, trying desperately to compose himself. He clasped them to his chest and took a deep breath. "I apologise. But please, I just . . . "

"Has something happened?" she asked. "Can I get you anything? A glass of water?"

He shook his head emphatically, droplets of sweat flying from his nose and chin. "Please. Just a taxicab. I want a taxicab. I want to leave."

She nodded as though she finally understood, but didn't reach for the phone. "The only problem is . . . you can't get a local taxi at this time. Midweek, they only run until one o'clock."

He glanced at the wall clock over her shoulder and saw it was almost 2:00 a.m. "Don't say that."

She gave him a sympathetic smile. "We are a little out in the wilderness, I'm afraid. I could try calling a city firm, if you like? It'll cost a little more, asking them to drive all the way out, but . . . "

He nodded. "Yes, please. Please do."

"All right," she said, finally picking up the phone. "The nearest, I think, is Fort William. They'll take about an hour to get here."

"An hour?" Heinrich very nearly shrieked. "I can't wait an hour! I don't have an hour!"

"Mr Stritzel . . . "

"Forget it," he cried, sounding hysterical. He waved his arms theatrically and started towards the door. "Forget it! I'll walk!"

"Mr Striztel," Mrs Dempsey called after him. "What about your room? Your bags? Mr Stritzel!"

He ignored her and kept walking, storming out through the door and down the steps, back into the night. The porch light barely illuminated a full yard of the path ahead. From then on it was solid darkness all the way to the main gate, beyond which a dim orange glow indicated the road and, beyond that, the distant comfort of civilization. Heinrich's eyes scanned the perimeter ahead, searching the shadows for signs of monsters.

It wasn't so very far to the road, he thought to himself. Not too far at all.

And so, leaving the dubious safety of the hotel and its porch light behind, he strode out into the darkness, marching quickly down the hill and into the car park. The soles of his shoes crunched loudly through the gravel, but he kept up his pace, eyes fixed on the main gate and the orange glow.

His gaze wandered as the path took him within view of the Ballador's rear garden. He glanced over to his right, wide eyes searching for signs of the creeping black weed and its gruesome spawn. All he could make out were a few leaves on the oak tree, their outlines painted white in the lights from the hotel.

"Hold it there."

Heinrich came to an abrupt halt, gravel scattering from his heels, at the sound of a woman's voice from directly ahead. He turned, squinted, and caught sight of her head and shoulders, black as pitch against the orange light. "Who's there?" he asked, keeping his voice low. "What do you want?"

"I want you to turn around and go back to the hotel." She spoke with an English accent, sounding authoritative and perfectly calm.

He let out a bitter laugh. "No, thank you. I've had quite enough of that place."

"I insist," she said.

"As do I. And I don't think you can stop me." He started forward, resuming his march.

The woman took a step towards him, raised her arm, and sent him sprawling to the ground. Her hand never touched him. They were still too far apart to make physical contact. Yet it was unquestionably her action that knocked him down, as though the air around her carried a weight and purpose all its own.

Heinrich scrambled back onto his feet, his face screwed up in fear and frustration. "Who are you? What do you want?"

"I want you to return to the hotel," she said as calmly as before.

"Please. Don't make me go back there." Tears welled up in his eyes. "Please, I beg you. Let me go. Please let me leave."

"No one leaves. It's already started. So you understand I *can't* let you leave. Now . . . return to the hotel."

Mrs Dempsey spun around at the slamming of the front door and saw Heinrich dart across the lobby. "Mr Stritzel?" she called.

He made it to the stairs and launched himself up them two at a time, knowing he had to find Gia and warn her. Teversham too, if he had the chance. He didn't know what he would say, couldn't be certain what was happening. All he could be certain of was that the net was closing in.

He was almost at the first floor landing, within sight of the Library Suite, when a figure manifested itself from the shadows before him. Heinrich came to another sudden halt, stumbling back at this latest obstruction. The figure strode out into his path, turned towards him, and then was gone. At the moment Heinrich stopped, it melted back into the shadows. He barely had time to register it. Not a woman this time. It had the vague features of a man, big and bulky, with the typical physical mannerisms of a bouncer. Heinrich instinctively deciphered it as a warning—an illusion conjured up by the same forces controlling the nightmares.

The message was clear. The Library Suite is off limits. Try to interfere and die.

Heinrich let his aching feet carry him back down the stairs and into the lobby.

"Mr Stritzel?" Mrs Dempsey's voice had a trace of genuine concern in it this time. She watched him as he came past, ashen-faced, eyes blank, staring into nothingness.

Twice defeated in almost as many minutes, and completely out of ideas, he went into the bar and ordered a large whisky. When Dennis served it, he thanked him, took it to a table in a quiet corner, and sat there with his head in his hands. "*Hier leg ich mich schlafen, Keine Nachtmahr soll mich plagen*," he muttered.

19

"I don't know what I'm doing here," Victor sighed. "I just don't know any more. I don't know . . . what I hoped I'd find."

Gia lay close beside him in the darkness, head on his shoulder, arm across his chest. "For me it was inspiration."

"For another show?"

She nodded. "And a little revenge. Do you know how much a week in one of these suites costs?"

"Uh . . . Yes, well, I think . . . I think so."

She laughed softly. "You see, to a man like you it doesn't matter. But trust me, it's far too much for someone like me. Back home, I was seeing a man. Or, more precisely, I was having an *affair* with a married man who I thought to be as interested in the darkness as I was. We talked about the Ballador a lot, its reputation, the dreams, the Residents. I thought it all had great potential for a show, but I knew that when he came here he'd be bringing his wife. So, on the day that I caught him with my best friend—the same day my show closed—I told him the only way I'd ever agree to keep my mouth shut would be if he let me have his reservation."

Victor felt a smile of admiration on his lips. "How very mercenary of you."

"He broke my heart," she said, very matter-of-fact. "I think . . . losing his reservation, getting put back on the waiting list . . . I think that broke his. I may have hurt him more."

"And your inspiration? Did you find that?"

She took a long, slow breath. "No. The first two nights in the Honeymoon Suite I didn't have any dreams at all."

He frowned. "But I thought . . . "

"It happens," she said. "They try to pretend it doesn't, but it does. I had no dreams the first night or the second, so I complained to the manager and she told me plainly. She said sometimes a guest is unconsciously resistant to the dreams, most usually in certain areas of the house. So she let me change my suite for this one. She guaranteed that every single person who had ever slept in the Library Suite suffered nightmares. And it worked."

"Here? This room?" he said.

She nodded, lowering her voice. "Victor . . . in all my nightmares, I only ever met one person."

He was silent, dreading her next words.

"It was you."

He was shaking his head almost before her sentence was complete. "No." He pulled away from her and sat up. "That can't be right." He turned on the bedside lamp.

"It was you, Victor," she repeated. He could see now there were tears in her eyes. "It was *you*. The things you did to me in those dreams . . . my God . . . " She winced in pain at the very recollection, hugging her arms about herself.

"I wasn't even *here* then," he cried, anger growing out of frustration.

"You *were*," she insisted. "In the dreams. In my head. The same way you got into other people's. It's the only way it makes sense."

"It's insane!"

"The first time was the night before you arrived. In the dream you called me a trespasser, a bitch, a fucking meddler who didn't understand the chaos she was causing. You told me to get the fuck out of this room. You told me to leave the hotel, and then you . . . you . . . " She was gasping, like there wasn't enough air in her lungs to form words.

"If I was so horrible," he asked, "why didn't you just leave?"

"Because I thought it was a fucking dream," she yelled,

Prince of Nightmares

loud enough to rattle the walls. "The next night, when you came to my door, if I'd had a gun I would have shot you. If I'd had a knife I'd have stabbed you. I was so fucking scared! So confused. And when next I slept, you hurt me, yes, but you didn't want me to leave any more because you needed me. You needed me to bring you here. If I'd left, you'd have stayed across the hall and that was no good, because you needed to be here. In this room. You had to be here or it wouldn't work."

"What wouldn't work? What the hell are you talking about?"

"You tell me!" Tears streamed down her face. "Tell me, Victor! I've done what you asked!"

"Jesus Christ." He left the bed and began picking his clothes up off the floor, pulling them on. "You're fucking insane."

"Maybe." She wept. "And that terrifies me too."

He zipped up his trousers. "I don't have any dark, mystical powers. Whatever anyone may have told you about me. I'm just a man."

"I know what I've seen. I know what you're capable of. I've felt it."

He shook his head and began buttoning his shirt. "You know nothing. I didn't even book the reservation. My wife did."

Gia stopped crying then. She raised up her head and regarded him with hard, almost pitying eyes. "Then she knew something about you that you didn't."

Victor flinched at that, the girl's words sending a chill through him, snuffing out any argument he might have made. Silenced, he looked away from her, picked up his jacket and headed out of the room.

"Victor," she said, a note of apology in her voice. "Victor, wait."

He ignored her, opened the door, and came face-to-face with a grinning man in a black suit. He recognised him immediately. Bald head, watery blue eyes and pale, stretched skin. The features were unquestionably his own. All except the grin. Victor had never grinned in such a way. No man could.

Gia screamed.

Victor opened his mouth to speak, but his opposite silenced him before he could utter a syllable, thrusting out a skeletal hand and punching into his chest. Thin fingers enclosed Victor's heart and squeezed, setting his blood on fire.

"And so," the man said, speaking through his teeth. "At long last."

Victor saw other creatures over his double's shoulder, more Residents crowding into the room, rushing to lay their own paws on Gia—who howled hysterically. There was nothing fetishistic about her fear now. Not amongst these demons.

Don't, he tried to say to them, without breath in his body or a pulse in his veins. *Please don't . . .*

He didn't see what they did to her.

In the next moment he was falling into darkness, away from the room, away from the hotel.

Life a bitter memory.

"Dazu helfe mir *Gott Vater, Sohn und heiliger Geist.* Amen."
The prayer finished, Heinrich unclasped his hands, took a sip
of whisky, and then began again. *"Hier leg ich mich schlafen,
Keine Nachtmahr soll mich plagen."*

Though he began in a whisper, with every recitation of
the charm, his voice grew louder. After he'd spoken it three
dozen or so times it became quite noticeable to the others in
the bar. Dennis, who liked a quiet life, had kept an eye on the
mud-spattered German, who seemed even more deranged
than normal, but was reluctant to approach him or make any
kind of enquiry as to his state of mind.

The young couple—the only other guests in the room—
managed to ignore him fairly well for a time, too wrapped up
in their own sleepy, half-drunk banter. But eventually they
too took notice and, once they'd done enough uncomfortable
glancing into Heinrich's corner and half-heartedly trying to
continue their conversation, chose to leave.

They finished their drinks, rose together, and walked
quickly out of the bar, heading for their room at the back of
the house. They passed Heinrich's table on their way, and
though they did their best not to make eye contact with him,
he noticed them, raising his head and fixing them with a
deranged gaze.

He stood, followed them out into the hall and watched
them turn the corner into the new part of the building. When
they'd retired to their room, he marched back into the lobby
and up to the front desk.

Mrs Dempsey was waiting for him, a practised smile on her face. "Yes?"

"You said there were rooms free in the extension?" He fired his words at her in a machine-gun whisper.

"Yes, I did," she said. "If you'd rather not return to your own room, I'd be more than happy to let you have one at no extra charge."

"No nightmares in those, correct?"

"That's right."

He nodded urgently. "The one furthest from the old part of the house. Can I have that?"

"Room 12, I think. Yes, it's free."

"I'll take it. I'll take it now."

"Very well."

She fetched the keys. He snatched them out of her hand, swapping them for the keys to his room on the second floor, then turned quickly about and strode off in the direction of the young couple.

"Shall I have Dennis bring your things down?" Mrs Dempsey called after him.

"That will be fine. *Danke schön*," he yelled in reply, without really listening to the question. He sped through the corridors at the rear of the house and down the long hall in the new building until he reached a dead end where the door to Room 12 stood.

He put the key in the lock, threw the door open, stepped inside, and slammed and bolted it behind him. After pulling at it a few times to check that it was secure, he went around the room and en suite switching on all the lights. Then he took off his coat, folded it, and pressed it tightly against the bottom of the door. That done, he took the Bible from the bedside table and began tearing the thin pages out, folding them and using them to plug up the rest of the gaps around the door's top and sides.

When he was satisfied the door was firmly sealed, he went to the windows and did the same for them. He checked the walls and skirting boards, then went into the en suite and plugged up all the taps and drains.

Every opening accounted for, he took what was left of the Bible to bed. He slipped off his shoes, curled up on the mattress, clutched the book to his chest and began again. *"Hier leg ich mich schlafen, keine Nachtmahr soll mich plagen."*

21

Victor knew even before he opened his eyes. He felt the weight of his limbs, gravity's familiar pull at his back and all the unbearable sensations that defined reality. And he knew. It had only been a dream. He was waking up.

Couldn't you tell? Don't you know the difference yet?

Opening his eyes only confirmed what he already knew. He found himself back in bed in the dimly lit Library Suite, Gia dozing softly beside him, her face peaceful and as perfect as a child's. At least he hadn't dreamed their tryst, or *hoped* he hadn't. It was all so difficult to tell these days. But the bubbling room, their argument, his demonic doppelganger at the door . . . all fictions, dredged up from his diseased subconscious. Dreams within dreams. And what evidence did he really have to say he wasn't dreaming now? That the past few days hadn't all been part of one long, elaborate nightmare fabricated specifically to drive him insane?

Shadows danced across the wall.

He bolted into a sitting position, head snapping left then right, scanning the room for signs of threats. Another flutter of movement caught his eye and he turned, ready to throw a fist into whatever phantom should come billowing towards him.

What he saw was a crane fly, about the size of his hand, perched on the shade of the bedside lamp. The movement of its stilt-like legs cast shadows on the walls.

Victor let his hands—which were balled up into fists—fall to his sides. He was very aware of his heart, which didn't seem to pound so much as oscillate. He watched the crane fly for a minute or more. Watched it shimmer, watched it blur. He didn't realise he was weeping until he felt the chill of evaporation on his cheeks.

His whole body began to shake as the tears took hold. He sank back down, into the bed, curling up on his side, thinking of Josephine and wondering if this, finally, was what she'd wanted. To torment him in the depths of his despair. To drive him past the brink.

Hardly a minute later he was weeping uncontrollably, face turned into his pillow for fear of waking Gia. The tears were hot and flowed like blood from a slashed artery. His chest and throat ached from his convulsions and futile attempts to contain them.

Is this madness? he thought. *Is that what this is? Am I mad?*

"No," Gia answered.

He turned back to her, wiping tears from his face. "What?"

"No," she repeated. Her eyes were closed, but they shifted beneath the lids. Her brow creased, angrily. "No," she murmured. "No . . ."

He relaxed a little. Just another dream.

"No . . ."

Mrs Dempsey showed Dennis a weary smile when he came back through to the lobby. "Mr Stritzel has moved to room 12. He's asked for his things to be brought down."

Dennis cringed. "Now?"

"I think it would be best. Don't want to give him another excuse to get upset."

"What if he's got a load of weird, kinky shit lying all over the place?"

She passed him the key. "Just . . . do your best."

He nodded and trudged reluctantly away.

With the lobby all to herself for the first time that

evening, Mrs Dempsey took off her glasses, sat down behind the desk, and bowed her head, hoping to rest her eyes for just a few minutes.

It occurred to Victor that he'd never actually seen someone in thrall to the dreams before. It seemed a useful experience. The kind of thing that might provide a little much-needed perspective. He shifted his position in the bed, getting a better angle as he watched Gia's tormented face, wondering what horrors she might be imagining. Could they possibly be as bad as his?

"No," She repeated, her brow creased, fingers twitching, head rolling from one side to the other. "No . . . "

Dennis halted when he reached the first floor landing and saw the door to the Honeymoon Suite was wide open. There was no one else in the hall.

He approached and called out. "Hello? Mr Teversham?"

No answer. No light from within. The open door presented a wall of black.

He edged a little closer, casting nervous glances back over his shoulder, unsure of exactly how far he should investigate. "Mr Teversham?"

He knew the man was old. Knew he'd been caught sleepwalking the night before. The Ballador did strange things to people sometimes. He'd seen it often enough before. Not sure how far to intrude, but knowing better than to ignore the signs that something was wrong, he crossed the threshold and was encased in shadow.

"Mr Teversham?" His words died on the air, swallowed up by the darkness.

The door swung softly shut behind him.

Victor observed Gia the way one might observe an

experimental test subject in a laboratory. He watched the nightmare take hold beneath her eyelids, grasp her mind and shake it, bombarding her with terror and depravity. The whole thing lasted less than five minutes.

"No." She sighed, becoming quieter now, the fit passing. "No . . . " A whisper. Her soft lips closed together. The fluttering movements in her features faded and she was silent.

Is that it? Victor wondered. *Is that all?* He placed his hand on her forehead and found it hot and wet. Her pulse raced. Her bare chest rose and fell with hurried breathing. Her small breasts quivered gently, beads of sweat running across her pale flesh.

He shook his head dumbly. All the terror the dreams had caused him, all the obsession . . . And for what? To the outside observer they were nothing.

He was turning away, disgusted, when something caught his eye. A movement that might have been shadow tracked across the top of Gia's left breast.

He peered a little closer and, as he watched, the nipple seemed to rise and darken. A small drop of ruby-red blood blossomed at the teat.

He caught his breath and extended a finger. The blood was wet, warm, and *real.*

Gia's eyes snapped open. "NO!"

The sound came like a wave crashing on the shore. Heinrich, at the furthest remove, could hear it coming. It started with a single scream. A young woman, far away in another part of the hotel. Gia, he imagined.

Very probably.

Victor could feel the dimensions of the room shifting, atoms expanding away from each other and suddenly, violently contracting. It felt like the same dizzying sensation he'd experienced in his suite before dinner, but multiplied a thousand fold. He reached out for Gia and saw her slide away from him, the same way his cuff links had. The same force sent him flying backward across the bed and tumbling to the floor.

He coughed and scrambled dizzily around, sheets coiled about and under him. When he was able to whip them off and look up he saw Gia, hovering a foot above the bed. Her eyes were wide. She screamed but seemed unable to move her limbs. Some unseen force had total control.

As Victor watched, an invisible claw took hold of her breast and crushed it; twisted it. Her arms bent back behind her head. Her fingers scratched uselessly at the wall. Her naked body arched upwards, her head rolling back. The force bent her farther and wrenched her legs apart. Violent spasms racked her pelvis and stomach as she was assaulted.

Victor pulled himself up onto the bed and made a grab for her, but the same phantom that held her knocked him away, sending him careening across the room to collide with the wardrobe. He collapsed into a useless pile among splintered wood and scattered clothes. "Stop it," he gasped, tasting blood in his mouth. "For Christ's sake . . . "

He felt vibrations in the floor, could hear pounding in the walls. From the other rooms echoed cries that more than equalled Gia's in pain and desperation.

Not nightmares. Not any more.

Mrs Dempsey jumped to her feet as the chorus of screams tore through the building. She spun about in a frightened circle, a cacophony of sound exploding from every room around her.

"Dennis?" she cried, barely able to hear herself over the noise. She put her hands over her ears. "Dennis!"

There was an explosion in the bar as every light went out, spraying blue sparks and broken glass across the room. Mrs Dempsey shrieked and ran around the desk, heading for the stairs. She was halfway across the lobby when she felt the floor beneath her begin to tilt.

She tried to maintain her balance, but the change happened too fast, the whole room shifting up at an angle, gravity taking a hold of her by the shoulder and tugging her down. She landed hard on her side as the bulbs burst in the lounge, casting the room into darkness.

Feeling a rumble in the building's foundations, a ringing in her ears, white spots in her sight, Mrs Dempsey pulled herself up onto her hands and knees and crawled for the stairs.

"Help," she cried. "Help me!"

Then the lights in the lobby exploded next and, in the darkness, she ceased to shout words, her screams becoming as base and animal as any other guest's.

Tears and sweat stained Gia's agonised face. Blood trickled from her mouth, where she had bitten her lip. There was blood around her broken fingernails, blood on her breasts, soaking her hair and on the sheets between her legs. Indentations marked the skin all over her body. It was as though imperceptible hands and instruments were tearing at her flesh—first from without, then from within. The skin over her belly contorted, spiking upwards. On her arms and thighs the flesh rippled and warped, like worms twisting through wet sand.

Victor lay shivering on the floor, useless as a frightened infant, trying to will his limbs into action, yet frozen to the spot. "Please," he gasped, his body quivering hopelessly.

He watched as the entity spun her, and then threw her body towards the wall. Tangles of brown hair came away from her head. Her frail young body shuddered and bent back. Her limbs were twisted unnaturally, grotesquely.

Victor closed his eyes against the sight, but soon opened them again when he heard the first bone snap.

John McNee

Heinrich was well used to all the sounds of torment, both within the walls of his own home and the walls of the Ballador, which weren't quite thick enough to mute the cries of guests in the depths of horror. So he didn't flinch when he heard Gia's voice howling down the halls, though he knew enough to recognise that it was different this time.

A moment later, several screams confirmed it. Male, female, other guests in other rooms. Mrs Forrester, Paul, Karen, and more. They began screaming one after the next, but didn't stop. It became a chorus of pain, carried down from the top floor, down and across, a virus spreading even to the rooms in the new part of the hotel. The guests who might reasonably have presumed themselves safe for the night. The young couples. The staff. They screamed. They all screamed.

Heinrich felt the room begin to shake, as though pistons were pressing at the walls.

His grip on the half Bible tightened. He repeated the charm.

And in the moment before all the screaming ceased, every light bulb in his room popped and went out.

"No," Victor moaned. "No, please . . . don't . . . "

They made knots of her limbs, fracturing the bones in a hundred places and forcing them into gruesome loops. Her ruined arms wound about her neck, strangling her. Victor thought she might pass out from the pain, but she didn't. She screamed. On and on, screaming without breath, until blood bubbled up her throat and out of her mouth, drowning her agonised sounds.

Victor looked on, unable to turn away, as her back broke and chest split, jagged ribs piercing the skin. Her blood was sprayed across the walls and furniture. The demons who held her were determined to crush her into a useless mass of skin and broken bones.

Gia's pale face shuddered, devoid of all emotion. Her eyes rolled back in their sockets and her bloodied head fell limply forward.

If he had hopes she was still alive they were extinguished a moment later as her ravaged belly burst, a red knot of entrails pouring out to splash on the carpet beneath her.

Her useless, compressed, eviscerated body hung pathetically in the air a moment longer, then dropped to the floor.

They were through with her.

Victor didn't move from his nest in the remains of the broken wardrobe. He clenched his fists and closed his eyes. *This is a dream,* he told himself calmly. *Just another stupid dream. Now is the time to wake up. Just wake up. Wake up.*

Wake up wake up wake up wake up wake up wake up wake up wake up wake up.

Evelyn Burgess had plenty of time to think and regret on the drive. Best guess said they could reach the Ballador in just over four hours, but Harry was keeping his foot down to make sure they got there sooner than that.

Damn Gallan. She blamed him when she wasn't busy blaming herself. Fergus McLoughty had been a good man who knew better than to go meddling with malevolence for personal gain. She knew he would have followed her instructions and boarded the Ballador up. She'd suggested he raze it to the ground, but even if he didn't do that much, she was certain he'd have made sure it remained empty for as long as he was alive.

Following his death, Gallan should have honoured his wishes and kept the house off the market. Evelyn could only surmise that the allure of money had overwhelmed his sense of duty.

She wasn't surprised by that. In recent decades, when she wasn't trying to forget all about the Ballador, she'd even guessed that he might try to sell it. The thought hadn't concerned her. After all, who would want to buy a house filled with nightmares? He'd never get it off his hands.

What she had never envisaged then, *could* never envisage, was the kind of world in which a property so steeped in evil could thrive as a gimmicky theme hotel for people with a lot more money—and unhealthy appetites—than sense.

When Harry told her, back at the house, she'd been stunned. "A *hotel?*"

"And a very popular one," he said. "Because it offers something no one else can."

Her face twisted in outrage. "Are people so stupid?"

"You better believe it. It's real popular among a certain crowd. There are waiting lists for some of those rooms."

"How long? I mean . . . how long has it been a hotel?"

He shrugged and produced his copy of the guidebook. "Over a decade. It's all in here."

She snatched it out of his hands. "What is this?" She thumbed through the pages, eyes widening as they lit upon the chapter headings and illustrations. "Insanity. This is nonsense. They've dressed it up like a ghost train. They've no idea. Absolutely no idea."

Harry sat back down opposite her. "Miss Burgess, please. I need your help." He held up the picture she'd shown him. "Josephine Morrison. The woman who was born in the Ballador's library. She grew up to marry my employer, Victor Teversham."

"Yes?"

"A few weeks ago . . . she killed herself."

Evelyn put a hand to her mouth. "I'm so sorry."

Harry shrugged it off. "Afterwards, we learned that on the same day she booked a vacation at the Ballador. That's where Victor is now. I've been putting this all together, forming a picture, forming some kind of answer to what it all means. But I'm not there yet, because I'm missing a vital piece of the puzzle. I need your help. I need you to tell me about the nightmares."

Evelyn stared down at the book in her hands. The look in her eyes was an even mix of sadness and fury. "They're not nightmares at all," she said at last. "That's just a disguise. They reach into your mind, cloaking themselves in unconscious thought and memories, so you might mistake them for something from your own head, but it's all a ruse. They present themselves as dreams to conceal their purpose."

"Which is what?"

"Escape."

Victor opened his eyes.

Gia's blood-smeared face peered up at him through a tangle of shattered fingers. Her mangled body didn't even twitch.

Not a dream.

The room, he realised, was still. Silent. The Residents' violent labour had passed and so they seemed at rest, for the moment. Victor tested his muscles and found he could move again. Whatever presence had held him in place had dissipated with the death of the girl.

Slowly, he dragged himself out of the ruined wardrobe and onto his feet. He staggered around to the side of the bed, pulled out one of the sheets, came back around and threw it over her.

It caught the air as it fell, billowing out like a white parachute, but imploded the moment the fabric touched her body, white fibres staining a deep, wet red and clinging to her flesh.

"I'm sorry," Victor said, and meant it.

He stood there a while, watching the seeping progress of her bodily fluids, lost in shock, not a coherent thought in his head. It was a few minutes before the fugue eased far enough to let him recognise the sounds of screams from across the hall.

He blinked, turned his head and listened. It sounded like a man in pain, crying for help.

Victor staggered towards the door and caught a glance of

his reflection in the dressing table mirror on the way. Seeing he was still naked, he doubled back, found his shirt and trousers and pulled them on. The screams did not abate.

Half-dressed, he left the bedroom for the sitting room and saw himself in a chair by the fireside. His double, smartly dressed in a black three-piece suit, scarlet tie and stiff collar, cross-legged and fingers steepled over his lap, grinned back at him.

Victor stayed where he was, held fast by fear and uncertainty, like a man who'd accidentally wandered into a lion's den. The figure in the chair didn't move, only watched and grinned.

When, after a minute or two, he still hadn't moved, Victor took a chance and strode quickly across the room, out of the door and into the hallway. The eyes of his double followed him as he left.

Out on the first floor landing, normalcy reigned—on the surface, at least. Peering up the stairs to the second floor, Victor could see nothing amiss, while a glance down to the lobby revealed only shadow. The lights in the stairwell flickered sporadically, but hadn't gone out. For a moment, Victor was stunned by how peaceful and quiet it was, seeming to invite him to forget the supernatural visions he'd witnessed. They didn't seem possible when confronted by such banality.

Then the screams began again.

Across the landing, the handle of the door to the Honeymoon Suite began to rattle. Someone pounded from the other side, apparently struggling to make their way out. Victor approached quite calmly and opened the door, then stepped back.

At first, the door only revealed darkness. Then Dennis came lumbering towards him on broken feet, howling like a tortured animal with each step. His body had undergone much the same punishment as Gia at the hands of the Residents. The front of his shirt was soaked in blood. With one mangled arm he was trying to hold a wound in his belly closed. His jaw was broken and hung limply, exposing rows of jagged shards that had once been teeth. He seemed to be making some attempt at speech, but all that issued from his mouth were vague moans, spit, and blood. His left cheekbone and eye socket had been crushed, so that the eyeball now dangled like a yo-yo on a string of nerve fibres. With his remaining good eye, still fashionably adorned with a ring through his eyebrow, he looked to Victor pleadingly, desperately, and held out a crooked arm in a begging fashion.

Victor stood his ground and watched, wondering what the young man could possibly expect of him. Did he want some kind of aid? Medical attention? He looked a touch beyond all that. Did he want sympathy? A witness to his deformity? Or just an explanation?

Victor could offer him nothing.

After an uncomfortably long silence had passed between them, the broken waiter turned away and hobbled off towards the stairs in search of someone who could offer him more. Victor watched him passively until he'd limped his way to the top step, at which point his broken feet betrayed him and he went tumbling down. His body smashed further with each painful impact, stair after stair, to land in a sprawling mess on the floor of the lobby.

Victor watched him as he lay there in a small pool of light at the foot of the stairs. He listened to him moan, watching as he squirmed on his stomach, a pool of blood spreading slowly out beneath him. He kept watching as long, thin fingers at the end of a yellow arm reached out from the shadows and clawed at the small of his back, digging deep into his flesh. Dennis's pained cries were already fading, whether from shock, loss of blood, or sheer hopelessness. They died to nothing as whatever was at the other end of the yellow hand gave a hard tug and dragged him away into the darkness.

Stepping back from the top of the stairs, Victor turned

toward the open door of the Honeymoon Suite and saw the Drowned Maid standing just within. She stared back at him without eyes, smiling without a face, basking in the glow of accomplishment, proud of the mutilation she'd wrought. His eye caught the suggestive curl of her tendrils, coaxing him back into the room.

He raised his hands, plaintively and politely declining her invitation, and ducked back into the Library Suite.

"Back so soon?"

He tensed at the sound of his own voice.

"How are things out there? Pretty fucked up, I'll bet."

Victor turned slowly around to face his double who hadn't moved from his seat in the armchair. "Who are you?" he asked once he found the strength to speak.

The man laughed. "Me? I'm the camel. And you are the eye of the needle. At least in this analogy." He uncrossed his legs and waved to the couch. "Why don't you come over here and have a seat and we'll talk it over? Pour yourself a drink, if you like."

Victor looked down and saw two glasses and half a bottle of red on the sideboard. The wine Gia had tried to tempt him with earlier. He felt a pang of guilt filling a glass, but the feeling dissolved when he knocked it back. He wiped his mouth with a shaking hand. "Who are you?" he repeated.

His double shrugged. "Is it a name you want? Visitors over the years have come to refer to me as the Master of the House. But if that's a little unwieldy I suppose you could always call me Mr Ballador." Again he motioned to the couch. "Now come sit down and I'll tell you the rest."

Victor stayed put a moment longer, swaying on his feet and trying to conceive a course of action that would get him out of the hotel with his life. Drawing a blank, he poured the rest of the wine into his glass, walked around the side of the couch, and took a seat.

"That's good, Victor," said Mr Ballador. "Good for you.

John McNee

Now I'm sure you want to know exactly what's happening here, but I hope you appreciate it's all a bit too complicated—and our time a little too limited—for me to really give you the full picture. There are always going to be holes. But I'm going to do my best to explain things as simply and as succinctly as possible. Because, I'll be honest, time really is of the essence here. All right?"

Feeling he should probably nod, Victor nodded.

"All right," said Mr Ballador. "Now, my friends and I . . . the ones you call Residents . . . There's a lot I could say about us. What I will say is this . . . we're not ghosts. We're not ghouls. We're not the envoys of the forces of darkness. What we are is a select group of individuals who, for a very long time, have wanted to come and play in your sandbox. For years we've tried and, for whatever reason, have never been fully able to make the transition. But we think now, finally, with your help, that aim can be achieved."

Victor swallowed. "With my help?"

"That's right. Your part is crucial in this, Victor. We need you."

"Need me? Need me for what?"

"To get out there. We need you to get us out of the hotel and into the world. We can't do it without you."

Victor nodded slowly. "And what will you do with the world . . . once you're out in it?"

Mr Ballador chuckled as though the answer was obvious. "We'll do whatever we like, Victor. Whatever we damn well please. And I include you in that, of course."

"Really?"

"Yes, it's like I said. We need you. It's like a partnership. You'll share our power. It'll take a little time, of course, but eventually, you'll be able to mould the world into whatever you want it to be."

"That's quite a proposition."

"You bet it is."

"But why me?" Victor asked. "Why am I being presented

with this honour? Who was it that decided I should be the one to inflict you and your kind upon the rest of humanity?"

Mr Ballador let the question hang in the air a moment, letting Victor believe he wouldn't answer or didn't have an answer. "Josie."

The name was like a knife in Victor's heart. "What?"

"Josephine began her life here, Victor. In this very room. She was conceived here and she was born here. For the time she was in the house she was like us. A vague idea still in gestation, all potential yet to be realised, yet to grow into a person. As such, she was the closest thing we had to an anchor in this world and our influence on her was more pronounced and more powerful than it ever was on anyone else . . . until tonight."

"I don't . . . I don't understand."

"But *she* did," said Ballador, leaning forward. "The first time I spoke to her she was still in the womb, but she heard. She understood. And when she left, she was on a mission. One that took most of her life to complete."

Victor felt sick. He gripped the sofa's armrest and closed his eyes, afraid the room was about to start spinning. "Oh, no," he moaned.

"You see," Ballador continued, "the reason we've been trapped here so long is that the partnership wouldn't work with just anyone. We've tried. That's what the nightmares are all about, but it would never work. It takes a very particular sort of man."

Victor opened his eyes. "I'm not an evil man."

Ballador made a quizzical face. "No, of course not."

"I'm not an evil man." Victor stood and began walking towards the door.

"I didn't say you were," said Ballador. "Victor, where are you going?"

He turned back at the door and hurled his glass across the room. It exploded a foot from Mr Ballador's face. The shards scattered out around him like raindrops. None touched him. "I'm leaving," Victor said.

Ballador shook his head. "You really shouldn't go out there. It's a bad time for it."

"Fuck you." He threw the door open, stepped out and slammed it behind him.

24

Victor stepped out of the Library Suite and into oil. It coated the floor from one side to the other, and soaked into the rug. His bare feet were painted in it the moment he stepped out. Oil ran down the walls and dripped from the ceiling.

They'd had the run of the place only a few minutes and already they were redecorating.

A sound filled the stairway—a low, snorting rasp, like a Clydesdale with a cold. He looked up as a grotesque giant lumbered into view on the top landing, dragging something behind him. He had a head of knotted, twisted scar tissue and wore an overcoat fashioned from blood and tar. In his left hand was a meat hook, skewering the ankles of a skinless, gurgling man who lay sprawled out and twitching on the floor behind him. It had to be, Victor knew, one of the top floor guests.

He turned away as the giant approached, launching himself down the stairs, not caring what other horrors awaited him, knowing only that he had to get out. His only plan—if it could even be called that—was to run and keep running, out through the front door and away from the hotel.

So he ran down the stairs, jumped the last three, landed in the lobby . . . and sank.

The floorboards had evaporated. He gasped as his legs disappeared into liquid, cold ink covering him up to his waist. It was difficult to see in the darkness, but intermittent flashes of electric blue highlighted enough for him to see the lobby was flooded. A pool of black stretched between him and the front door.

There were other shapes in the gloom, lit all too briefly for him to discern what they were. They moved. Flickering jumbles of dark meat and blade, darting through the shadows. They had the grace of cockroaches, skittering out of sight. He heard them more clearly than he saw them. Heard their slicing metal movements and tinned, static laughter.

Ignore them, he told himself. *Keep moving. Don't look back. Get out. Go.*

He rushed forward through the ink and found the floor beneath yielded to his foot. He was treading on flesh. He threw out his arms to steady himself, but there was nothing to hold on to. Ice-cold ink splashed up his spine as he sank deeper, his foot coming down once more to find more skin, tougher this time. There was bone beneath it.

As he moved slowly onwards, fighting against his revulsion, he began to recognize the body parts under his feet. He trod on backs and elbows, shoulders and breasts, scalps and faces. Long wet hair clung to his shins. His toes slid against closed eyes and into open mouths. There were dozens of bodies beneath him, knotted together in the ink, which grew deeper with each passing tread. He quivered with the cold as it rose up to his belly, then to his chest, then came lapping against his collar-bone.

The darkness was now too pronounced for him to see the entrance, but he knew it couldn't be far. He couldn't see his own arms, but he held them out in front of him, groping through the black, hoping to find the means to his escape.

Behind him, from the stairs, echoed an awful scream. *Don't look back*, he told himself. *Don't look back.* The scream rose in pitch and volume, unidentifiable as male or female. He pressed on, surely past the front desk by now, almost at the door, ink up to his chin. "Don't look back," he whispered. "Don't look back."

Prince of Nightmares

"Mr . . . Teversham?" The voice came from directly ahead. He halted, toes kicking against a leathery torso, nearly treading water. "Who's there?" He could see nothing.

"It's the manager, Mr Teversham. It's Mrs Dempsey." Her voice was weak, barely recognisable, as though she were being gently strangled.

"Where are you?" he whispered. "I can't see you. Can you give me your hand?"

"No," she replied, with aching sadness. "I don't think I can. I think . . . I must have fallen asleep."

"What's that?" He reached out his arm towards her voice.

"I know this isn't real," she said. "I know I must be dreaming. But I can't seem to wake up."

There was a sound all around them, like the snapping of ten thousand fingers, and then light. A radiant white beam from an unknown source exploded the darkness and lit up everything throughout the ground floor. Victor threw up his arm as a shield against the glare, blinking as things began to take form in his vision.

A moment later, his stinging eyes had grown accustomed to its brilliance and he saw the woman before him as she really was.

"Jesus," he moaned.

They'd unravelled her like a ball of twine, picking at a vein and teasing it until it all came apart. Her flesh had been pulled across the entrance—a red portcullis of stretched muscle and sinew. Her feet were pinned in the bottom corners, hands pinned at the top, tendons snaking out of each like threads for the loom. Her organs, dotted across the tapestry, hung like bunches of grapes on the vine, still quivering with the pulse of life. In the midst of it all, raised up in a hammock woven from intestines and stomach lining, was her head. Her face was pallid, drained of blood. Her sunken eyes stared down at him from under her helmet of still vibrant orange hair.

"Please," she said. "I'd like to wake up."

He couldn't bear to look her in the eye. He turned away, took a step back and felt his foot slip from its perch.

Before he could cry out, his head was under and he was sinking fast. He kicked and tried to swim back to the surface, but hadn't moved as much as an inch before cold hands clawed out of the darkness, grasping at his leg and wrenching him down into the void.

He shrieked through bubbles of black, eyes widening in fright as ink splashed into them, blinding him. He lashed out with his arms and kicked again as other hands grasped for him, bodies swarmed him, pressed their cold dead skin to his.

He thrashed without sight, deaf to everything but his own blood in his veins, pulse racing, heart threatening to explode if he couldn't catch a lungful of air.

The arms of drowned corpses twisted their way around him like rope, tying him up in chains, weighting him down, dragging him to a cold death. All the energy he could muster wasn't enough to shake even one of them clear. He didn't have the strength to fight them off. He knew that.

And maybe it was sheer desperation coupled with the hopeful hallucinatory madness that comes from facing certain death that brought to mind Heinrich's talk of willpower. Blind, deaf and drowning, his limbs locked, Victor knew his will was all he had left.

It was worth a shot.

25

He opened his eyes to find he was sitting at one end of a long, dark table in a room obscured by fog.

His head ached. His nostrils were filled with the scent of blood and rotting fish.

On his right sat Paul. He seemed deep in thought, all the muscles in his bearded face clenched, as though he were trying desperately to remain in control.

"Paul?" Victor heard someone say, not sure if it was him.

The scrawny little man shuddered fitfully and screamed. On the opposite side of the table, Karen laughed. Victor turned to look upon her. She laughed fiercely and clearly, though her mouth had been sewn shut. Her chest and stomach swelled and pulsated. Her puffy limbs seemed broken and useless. They dangled pathetically at her sides.

Her husband yelped a second time and she smashed her head down on the table. When she sat upright again her forehead was smeared with blood. Her widening eyes looked to Victor for help. She was afraid and plainly in tremendous pain. He could do nothing.

Paul yelled again, juddered violently and stabbed his fingers into his eye sockets. Black blood jetted out over his hands and down his face. He screamed with the pain, but only dug farther, squashing his eyeballs with his fingers and tugging them free. The mashed pink lumps landed on his place mat in a pool of blood. His hands probed deeper into the empty sockets, tearing away flesh and gore, and then digging away at his nose and the skin on his cheeks. He scratched and tore at his face until it was all sitting in a shredded wet mess before him. He turned towards Victor and displayed the gaping crater where his eyes, nose, and mouth had been moments before. Paul pressed his hand into the mess, groped around and produced a long, silver blade.

On Victor's left, Karen battered her face against the table a second time. He looked to her and saw that the blood vessels in her eyes were breaking. Saw, too, the stitches over her nostrils. They had been sewn shut. She couldn't breathe. Her throat bulged and stretched in monstrous fashion. And still, somehow, her laughter echoed.

Faceless Paul swung the blade across the table and sliced open the stitches that held Karen's mouth shut. Dark liquid sprayed out from her lips and drenched the table. Her mouth opened wide and what looked like her tongue—long and black—snaked out. It hit the table with a wet thud. An eel. A second followed, slithering up her throat to land, quivering, by its brother. Karen vomited up a third and a fourth and more, until the table and floor were covered in writhing, black fish.

One of the eels came flopping pathetically towards Victor, turning its broad head his way and mouthing silent pleas with its fleshy lips. Victor recoiled as it approached, feeling the bile rising at the back of his throat.

"Always hated eels, haven't you Victor?"

He looked up and saw Mr Ballador at the other end of the table, limping through the fog, one fist gripping the silver handle of Victor's walking cane. What he said was true enough. Victor had hated eels since childhood. The revulsion he felt at the sight of them eclipsed the disgust most people felt at the sight of spiders or rats. Yet even that paled into significance compared to his feelings for Mr Ballador.

"Monster. You fucking monster!"

"No, no, no," Ballador said, his tone relaxed and even. "You can't blame me for this. This is all you, my friend. All of it."

"What?"

"Muddy thinking." Ballador tapped a finger to his temple. "You let your subconscious have the run of the place and look what happens. Sheer bloody chaos."

"I didn't do this," Victor said, waving a furious hand at his mutilated dinner guests. Karen didn't move any more. Her head hung back, over the chair, her distended neck bulging every so often to announce the emergence of yet another slippery eel. Across from her, Paul's faceless head sank down to land on the table. He was still. "There's no way I did this!"

"You saved yourself from drowning," Ballador said. "That was clear thinking. But you need to maintain focus. Otherwise all your fears and insecurities take over. They manifest themselves and wreak havoc. Now, I can teach you how to do it. I'd *like* to teach you."

"Teach me how to kill? Teach me how to murder the fucking world?"

Ballador shook his head. "You've got me all wrong, Victor. I'm here to *save* the world, not murder it. And I haven't killed *anyone.*"

"Liar!" Victor spat. "You killed Gia! You tore her to pieces in front of me. You can't accuse me of that. No way. I'd have saved her. I'd have . . . have . . . "

Ballador held up his hands in mock surrender. "All right. All right. Calm down. There's no need to get upset. You're right. You weren't responsible for what happened to her. Only . . . she's not dead."

"Fuck off."

Ballador grinned. "Birth, by its very nature, is a violent process. It's painful and it's bloody. Everything you've seen tonight is part of the process. Unavoidable. But I'm not here to kill, Victor. I'm here to extend life. Enrich it."

As he spoke, Paul and Karen jolted back into the waking world, resuscitated by his voice. Paul immediately put his hands to the hole where his face had once been, felt around its edges, then began searching the table for the pieces he'd torn off.

"What the fuck are you talking about?" Victor barked as Karen toppled from her chair, resurrected to writhe on the floor among the eels.

"What I'm offering you is a chance to change things." Ballador's eyes flashed. "Life, death . . . it doesn't have to be the way it is. We can redraw the map. We can remake the world. And we can start with Gia. You just need to let me show you how."

The intervening minutes or hours—Victor had no idea how long it had been—hadn't worked any miracles on Gia's corpse. She lay where he'd left her, a miserable pile of gore hiding under a blood-soaked bedsheet, like something a butcher might leave out for the dogs. One twisted foot jutted out from the corner—skin blotchy with purple bruises, toes broken, toenails bent back at aggressive angles—illustrating just a fraction of the horrors wrought upon her.

"She looks pretty dead to me," Victor said.

"Yes," Ballador agreed, prodding her with his cane. He smiled at the sound it made, like poking a sack of rotted fruit. "It'll take some doing to get breath back in her, but I reckon you're up to the task."

"She angered you, didn't she?" Victor wasn't as close to the body, standing with his back to the door, keeping his distance.

Mr Ballador shrugged and wandered around the side of the bed. "A spanner in the works, that's all. She was in the wrong place. We needed you in this room. That's just the way it had to be and how it would have been. But then she moved in." He paused at the bedside table, eyes on the crane fly which lay dead and desiccated on its surface. "We've waited fifty years for this moment, Victor, so I hope you can appreciate my frustration. Yes, I took it out on her, but at the time I wanted her out. Then you arrived, which called for a change of tactics."

"That all sounds very pragmatic," said Victor. "But what I'm looking at is a bunch of guts on the floor."

Ballador sighed and rubbed a liver-spotted hand across his forehead. "You *will* understand, Victor. Eventually. I promise you that. But right now, how about we just focus on the girl?"

Victor couldn't imagine what he'd experienced would ever make sense to him, but he was willing to set it to one side for now. He took a deep breath. "Show me what to do."

Ballador nodded enthusiastically. He gathered the dead crane fly in his handkerchief and put it in his pocket, then limped back to Victor. "Very simple, really. It's all in the eyes. If you see it, you can change it. Remember that. Now, take a step to the left. That's good. Straighten up. Close your eyes. I want you to picture her as she was. As you want her to be again. Can you do that?"

Victor thought again of descending the stairs for dinner, seeing her below him. Brown hair curled and pinned in place, bright eyes framed by darkness, soft skin wrapped in a dress of deep, dark red. Remarkable to think it had only been a few hours ago. "Got it."

"Good." Ballador put a hand on his shoulder. "Now look at her. And remake her as she was."

Victor let a gust of air out of his lungs before he opened his eyes, and then fixed them on the crumpled red-brown heap on the floor in front of him. Immediately the vision of her in his head shattered, but he fought to reclaim it, trying to imagine her in front of him as she had been. Better than that. Not imagining. *Seeing.* He wanted to *see* her.

The pile moved. A sudden crinkle in the sheet, a twitch of dead tissue. Victor blinked.

"Don't blink," Ballador whispered at his ear. "Don't lose focus. See it. Change it. It's as simple as that."

Victor swallowed hard, eyes wide, sweat on his brow. "See it." Her exposed foot began to inch back across the carpet, slipping under the sheet. "Change it." A muffled pop announced the successful insertion of an arm back into its socket. It was followed by a succession of crunches and cracks as contorted limbs unwound, joints realigned and bones rudely snapped back into place.

"That's it," Ballador said, watching keenly as Gia's body slid up into a sitting position, then slowly—as though being pulled by marionette strings—stood up.

The sheet dropped down from about her head, which hung limply forward, face hidden by hair matted with blood. Victor lifted his gaze and her body came with it, raised up a foot or so into the air. The ragged hole in her abdomen stretched wide to welcome back her entrails, which unspooled like a dancing cobra from their coil on the floor and slithered up inside her.

It was like putting a broken doll back together and just as inexact a science. Victor didn't have the medical knowledge to know where everything went. He could only pack her organs back inside her and seal the wound, straighten her broken limbs and smooth out the bumps under the skin. He could mould her, but he couldn't heal her. The bloody bedsheet wound its way around her torso and over her hips, making for a poor imitation of her red dinner dress, while concealing the worst of her deformity.

Victor knew he was done, knew he could do no more, as he set her back down on her reconstituted feet. Looking at her, he felt ashamed of the effort.

Mr Ballador patted him on the back. "Ah, close enough."

Gia's head jerked up, hair flying back and bloodshot eyes popping wide as she sucked air down her throat in a long, hungry gasp. She threw a hand up to her chest, stumbled back, hit the wall and stayed there, using it to prop herself up. She took another gasp of air, gagged, bent forward and hawked a thick wad of congealed blood onto the carpet.

"Gia?" Victor took a single, tentative step towards her, but was wary of getting any closer.

"Fuck," she spat, thick strings of scarlet saliva still

hanging from her lips. She straightened up and held her hands out in front of her, eyes roving over her crooked fingers, blood-caked skin, and pronounced purple veins. "Victor," she moaned. Her voice had lost all its youth, becoming the guttural croak of an emaciated old woman. Bloody tears welled up in her eyes. "What the fuck have you done to me now?"

26

"**She hates me**," said Victor.

"She'll come around," said Ballador. "Just wait and see."

The two of them stood in the Library Suite's sitting room, Ballador by the fireplace, Victor at the window. He was staring out at a tangled web of thick black weeds. It seemed to be covering the entire building, blocking all the exits, keeping everyone trapped inside. He could still hear screams echoing through the walls. Elsewhere in the hotel, the Residents kept up their assaults.

"You're a novice," Ballador said. "You were never going to get her looking exactly right the first time. The point was to get her up and about again." He took the handkerchief from his pocket, opened it out, and flipped the dead crane fly into the flames.

"What's that?" Victor asked, watching the reflection in the window.

"Just an old soldier who's served his purpose," Ballador said and turned. "Look, don't worry about Gia. When you've had a bit more practice, you can take another crack at her, fix her up properly. Hell, she can do it herself eventually. Soon she'll be able to make herself look and sound however she pleases. Presuming everything goes well."

"That's why you look like me? Sound like me?"

Ballador nodded. "It just makes the transition easier. Right now we look like each other and sound like each other. All goes right, by morning we'll *be* one another, united, sharing the same mind. The same body. The same power."

Prince of Nightmares

Victor looked from Ballador's reflection to his own. "I won't be myself anymore."

Ballador smiled. "You say it like it's a bad thing. Besides which, we'll both be making sacrifices. For my own part, I'm giving up what could've been a millennia-long reign as the crown prince of nightmares, but hey, it's like the song says . . . " He snapped his fingers and kick-shuffled his feet in a half-hearted imitation of a foxtrot, singing, "*I'd rather beeee the girl in your arms than the girl in your dreams . . .* "

Somewhere in the dark recesses of Victor's mind a voice said, *That's it. That's the song.* "I've heard some sales pitches in my time . . . "

"Honestly, Victor!" Ballador threw up his hands in frustration and collapsed into his armchair, as though the exertion of his seconds-long dance had completely worn him out. "Stop looking for catches that aren't there. This is the one chance you get to make every dream a reality. Literally! Are you resisting just because you can? Just because you think you ought to? Because I tell you now, there are millions who'd bite my arm off for what I'm offering."

"Take it to them then," Victor yelled back, finally stepping away from the window and turning to face him.

"I can't," Ballador answered through gritted teeth. "And don't pull the meek and humble act with me, boy. We both know better. Truth is, I'm not offering anything you haven't desired, haven't *craved* for as long as you've been alive. What else has your life been about but the accumulation of wealth, the strive for power? Even with all you had you never stopped. Never slowed. Never paused to question why however much you had, you always needed more. That's the kind of man you are, Victor. Now I'm here, offering you immortality and you have the gall to pretend it doesn't excite you? We can reshape the boundaries of reality. For fuck's sake, we can live forever! You've felt it yourself. A couple of days ago you were a miserable old man—a shell of a man on the edge of death. Now look at you! Scaling mountains and fucking models. And all you've had is a taste."

Victor suddenly broke into a fit of hysterics—couldn't help it—and covered his face with his hands. "I can't believe I'm having this conversation," he moaned through the laughter. "Jesus Christ, help me."

Ballador raised an eyebrow. "Don't ask him for help. You'll be a long time waiting. Are you quite finished?"

Victor was wiping tears from his eyes. He sat down on the arm of the sofa. "I didn't ask for this."

Ballador leaned forward, craning his neck to make eye contact. "But you *want* it, don't you?" Every line in his face was highlighted by the flames in the fireplace. He looked more the Devil than ever.

Victor, giving the question serious thought for the first time, shook his head. "I don't know. Maybe it was the striving I enjoyed. Does anyone really want to be reality's master? Sounds like a poisoned chalice if ever I heard one."

"Bullshit," Ballador spat. "That's the talk of the privileged and guilty. Do you remember that part of the Bible where God, finally realising the burdens of such limitless power, gives it all up so that he may live, struggle, suffer, and die like an ordinary mortal?"

Victor frowned. "No."

"No," said Ballador. "Because that would be fucking ridiculous. Creatures like us don't suffer guilt, Victor. Nor do we suffer boredom, nor hunger nor . . . fucking *suffering*. We transcend this miserable void for a higher plain of existence. Try and explain to me one more time how this is a bad deal. You gain more than you can possibly conceive. And all it costs you is . . . "

"My humanity?"

Mr Ballador scoffed at the melodrama. "Oh, Victor, please. We both know you had precious little of that to begin with."

Prince of Nightmares

Gia slipped out of the suite while the two were arguing. Victor had his back to her, so didn't notice. Mr Ballador saw her, but only smiled and politely nodded his head as she quietly opened the door and darted through it.

She stepped out onto a floor of wet leather littered with bottle caps, chicken bones, and shards of glass. The walls around her were constructed from thin black plastic, barbed wire, and balsa wood. They billowed in the breeze that drifted up the stairwell, carrying clouds of brown vapour and a scent of sweat and cinnamon.

Fears—conscious and subconscious—permeated the air like gas, warping the fabric of the building, mutating her surroundings into a confused, ugly jumble.

She crossed the landing—not caring or even feeling as glass sliced through the soles of her feet—and descended the stairs, knowing the scene would have transformed completely by the time she returned.

The lobby was suffering the same fever-dream symptoms—a dimly-lit jungle of slate and sheet ice, honeycomb, and exposed wire. Staring through the mist and chain-link barricades she could see the shimmering black-red back of the Giant. He was hard at work, driving slivers of rusty metal into the flesh of two skinless guests, strung up by their feet. The Giant knew how to make the most of the limited time available to him, focusing on areas that would yield the greatest reward—the spaces between their toes, the base of the spine, the pink, exposed gums. Gia imagined it had to be awfully difficult to scream when your mouth was full of needles. Somehow, his victims managed.

She watched the show for a minute or so, then wandered into the lounge bar where Mrs Forrester lay, writhing on the floor. She was wearing a lace nightgown, only lightly dappled with blood and her blonde hair, damp with sweat, clung to her neck and shoulders. She was curled up on her side, one leg kicking out at an angle, hands gnarled like claws, tension in every muscle. Her face was a deep shade of sunburn red, eyes bulging and bleary, teeth gritted against the pain, though Gia couldn't tell exactly what was wrong with her.

It was only when she bent down to take a closer look that she spotted the lumps moving under her skin. The Swarm was in her veins. Tiny red pockmarks all over her arms and legs showed the places where they'd burrowed into her flesh, just deep enough to insert themselves in her blood stream. Now they crawled the length and breadth of her, tiny black bodies burning her from the inside out.

When she'd grown tired of watching Mrs Forrester, Gia turned away, kicking a path through pieces of Dennis to reach his head and torso at the bar. He lay face up on its surface, arms gone, legs gone, gurgling through bubbles of blood and vomit, unable to speak, unable to save himself, unable to die.

The Crab sat prone above him. A naked female, this one, with a bald head and body made of double joints and right angles. Her yellow arms were elbow deep in Dennis's rib cage, carrying out a vivisection with her thin fingers. He stared at Gia with his one eye, mouth opening and closing in breathless desperation. She ignored him and continued on, past the dining room—where Paul and Karen endured the latest icicle inventions of the Crystal Mistress—and into the extension.

The corridor in the new part of the building was disguised as a brick sewer tunnel. Gia navigated puddles of piss and liquid shit as she passed one occupied room after another. Through the open doors she caught glimpses of more Residents, more guests, all engaged in the exhausting business of post-mortal mutilation.

The scene behind her was already twisting into a new configuration as she reached the room at the furthest end of the hotel, raised her fist, and politely rapped on the door.

No answer.

Prince of Nightmares

She tried again. "Heinrich? Hello? It's Gia."

There was muffled noise from within, like he was scrambling through darkness to reach the door. "Who is it?" he whispered. "Who's there?"

"It's Gia, Heinrich. Could you let me in please?"

"No," he replied. "No. NO! Go away!"

She looked over her shoulder at the churning sewer tunnel, lit in industrial fluorescent orange. "I'd much rather come in."

"I lay me here to sleep, no nightmare shall plague me . . ."

She rolled her eyes. "Oh come *on*, Heinrich! I'm not a nightmare. I'm Gia!"

"Prove it!"

"How the fuck am I meant to prove it, Heinrich? I am me. I just am! What else can I do?"

"You sure?" he said, voice tremulous with fear. "I mean . . . you're sure you're you?"

She glanced down at her pulverised and repackaged body, bandaged with the bedsheet. "About as sure as I can be, yes."

"You swear it?"

She laughed. "Yes, Heinrich. I swear. For whatever that's worth."

He was silent for a few moments. "I want to believe you."

She rested her forehead against the door and lowered her voice. "Heinrich, please. It's not much fun out here right now and I've no one else to talk to. I swear I'm me. I swear I won't hurt you."

Another long moment of silence. "All right. All right. I'm going to open the door. Just for a moment."

She grinned and felt the skin split around her mouth. "A moment should be plenty."

27

"Escape?" said Harry. "You think they can do that?"

"I don't doubt it," Evelyn answered. "But they'd need help."

"What do you mean?" Harry's voice rose in frustration. "What *are* they?"

"I can't be as exact as you want me to be. I don't know how to explain it."

"You can tell me. Tell me and I'll believe it. Ghosts? Demons? The forces of Hell?"

"Yes. All of that. And no, none." Evelyn cringed. "Just . . . bad ideas."

"What?"

She sighed. "It's like . . . It's like cultivating plants."

"Okay."

"Say you wanted to grow a tropical plant of some kind, which, incidentally, is very difficult to do in this part of the world. You first need to create the right conditions. The right temperature, soil, nutrition, sunlight. PTR is like that. Geographically problematic. Projected thoughts won't flower in the wrong conditions. Cold reality kills it dead. And so the Ballador was like our greenhouse. We made a perfect bubble where the atmosphere was warm and pliable, where our thoughts could take form and thrive. And thrive they did. But so did the weeds. We never prepared for the weeds."

"And where did the weeds come from?"

Her smile was desperately sad, almost ashamed. "From the same place as the flowers, of course. From the earth. From *us*."

Prince of Nightmares

"You're saying you invented them?"

"No. Invention implies intent and there was no intent. What they are . . . " She glanced down at the guidebook still open in her hand. "The *Residents* are the parts of ourselves we wanted to keep hidden. The parts we didn't like. The parts we suppressed. Invasive thoughts, base urges, and hateful impulses. They are the worst possible versions of ourselves, emboldened by our fear of things beyond our conception. Sadistic, spiteful, greedy, and utterly merciless. All of the evil. None of the good."

"You're serious."

She nodded. "There's no such thing as Hell, Harry. It's a human concept. The problem with the Peter Project was that it made concepts a reality, even if you didn't want them to be."

Harry scowled, rubbing a hand across his brow. "Ghosts I could have maybe wrapped my head around, but this?"

"It's so much worse than that," she said. "Evil isn't an alien thing. It exists in the minds of every man and woman. But the world has never seen such purity. While we slept, our demons escaped. Like weeds through the soil. They took form in the shadows and nourished themselves on our dreams. I don't know how long we lived like that, sharing the house with them. Only after the nightmares began, once we saw them for ourselves, did we recognise them."

"So you knew even then they weren't just dreams?"

Her sparkling eyes lingered on the guidebook. "They might fool others but not their mothers." The corner of her mouth twitched, almost forming a smile. "I have a feeling we used to sing something like that at school."

"Evelyn."

The smile vanished, replaced by a sombre, almost shameful expression. "Ghosts. Demons. Weeds. We each sired one. It's not an inversion, not like a mirror image, nothing so cleanly defined, but we recognised them. For all the disguises they wore, all the different faces, we each recognised a part of ourselves. They learned how to manipulate their image very quickly. And how to sustain themselves. Very fast learners, all of them, I'll admit. I can't imagine how far they might have evolved since. "

"You ran," Harry said.

She nodded. "We did. Knowing they couldn't follow, not without anchors in the real world. We disbanded the group and scattered, so it couldn't happen again. I thought they might wilt and die, left alone in the Ballador. But of course he's smarter than that."

"He?"

She tapped her finger on the open page, the picture of a pale man in a dark suit. "I dreamed of the Devil. And so he came to be."

Harry was quiet for a long time, trying to process what she was saying. Dozens of questions presented themselves, but one loomed large over the rest. "What do they want?" he asked.

She gave him a curious look. "Isn't it obvious? They want exactly the same thing we did. They want to change the world."

A short time later, Harry made his call to the Ballador. When that failed, he said he would drive. He couldn't sit still, couldn't go back to his own hotel, and certainly didn't intend to wait around for Victor to check out. He would go there now, hoping to arrive before the dawn.

"I'll come with you," she said, dismissing his protestations. "I need to see it for myself."

Harry stopped the Bentley at a service station to get petrol. He filled the tank to the brim, then opened the boot, took out a green jerry can and filled that too. Evelyn tried to tell him there was no need. She said a full tank would be more than enough to get them to the Ballador and back. But Harry believed in being prepared. He thought that once they got Victor there would be no more stopping for gas. He planned to put his foot down and keep it there until they reached the airport.

So she left him to it, standing off at the other side of the car, making the most of the opportunity to stretch her seventy-nine-year-old legs and staring out across the darkened landscape. She turned back as he was loading the jerry can back into the boot and only then did she see it.

The car had been hired in Glasgow, so there wasn't the usual assortment of forgotten belongings and bric-a-brac you'd find in most car boots. Only a small suitcase, Harry's folded overcoat and, nestled between the two, a small black revolver in a leather holster.

She didn't bring it up until they were back on the road. After driving for ten minutes or more in silence, she looked at him. "How long have you worked for Victor Teversham, Harry?"

"Twenty-six years," he answered immediately.

"My goodness. That's a long time."

"I guess."

"And what exactly is it you do for him?"

He smiled. "It'd be quicker if I told you what I *don't* do for him."

"I see. His man Friday?"

"Something like that. I do my best to keep his life running as smoothly as possible. I keep people out of his way that he doesn't want to talk to. I get him what he wants, wherever we go, even if it's hard to get. I've always been good at that. I make travel arrangements, set up meetings, manage his people, monitor security—"

"You're a bodyguard."

"Among other things."

"So you carry a gun."

"Mostly. It depends where we are. You have to abide by the law of the land, so depending which country we're . . . " He let the sentence trail off. "You saw the one in the trunk, didn't you?"

"It may have caught my eye," she admitted. "Not something I'm used to seeing. What with them being illegal and all."

"You don't need to worry about that."

"Don't I?"

"Look." He sighed. "Victor is worth just short of one billion dollars, okay? He's involved in energy, pharmaceuticals, and weapons. He's got to go to a lot of dangerous places and talk to a lot of dangerous people. And he's got enemies. Ideally he'd have an army looking out for him twenty-four-seven, but you can't trust a whole army. So he's got me."

"And he can trust you, can't he?"

Harry said nothing, apparently insulted by the question.

Evelyn sat and watched him for a few moments. There was more she could have said, more questions she could have asked. Questions about duty. Questions about guilt. Questions about how much he would have been willing to do not for Victor, but for Josephine Teversham, when she was alive. Instead, she turned to the window and stared out at the night as it passed them by.

28

In the darkness, Gia's thumb brushed against a stray scrap of skin hanging from the cuticle of her index finger. She gripped it between the thumb and forefinger of her other hand and pulled, tearing off a long strip down to the knuckle. It didn't hurt. She kept pulling and teased away more skin, past the knuckle, over the back of her hand, stopping only when she reached the wrist. It didn't even sting. She felt the air on exposed muscle, the wetness of blood as it leaked from the wound. But it didn't hurt.

She was long past the point of pain.

"Do you know what they're doing out there?" she asked, raising her voice above the cries of anguish from other rooms.

"Hurting people," Heinrich answered. He was on his knees at the door, folding Bible pages to plug up the cracks. "Torturing them. I don't know why they don't just kill them."

"They're not going to kill them, Heinrich. They need them alive. They need their pain. They feed on it. They sow, reap, and consume pain. A harvest of suffering that soon the world will know." She smiled as she said it. "But what they're doing right now is conditioning."

"Is what?"

"Conditioning," she repeated. "Pain sharpens the mind. You ever hear that? Torture a man until you break him—pull his toenails out, pour capsicum in his eyes—and he'll confess to crimes he didn't commit. Push him far enough and he'll *believe* it. That's what they're after right now. They need minds that are both lucid and compliant. And they're getting it the only way they know how."

"Try not to be afraid," he said, misinterpreting her emotional state. "We can survive this."

"Are you so sure?"

"We just need to stay here—right here—until dawn and we'll be all right."

She frowned, though he couldn't see it. All he'd seen of her was a blur through the doorway and a shadowy outline in his unlit room. The fact had saved her some explanation. "You think the dawn will save us?"

"Of course," he said with total certainty. "The dawn brings other staff. Other guests. Families and friends wondering where their loved ones are, why they won't answer the phone. Eventually, it brings policemen, ambulances, the army even."

"I don't think any of that will make a difference. He'll be unstoppable by then."

"Who?"

"Victor."

"What's Victor got to do with any of this?"

"He's upstairs now, talking things over with the Master of the House. I think they're going to go into business together."

"What are you talking about? Gia, I don't understand!"

"Victor's responsible for all this. He's the one who brought them out of the dreams. They're forming a union so that they can all leave the hotel together and start reshaping the world."

"A union?"

"I expect it will be a beautiful ceremony."

"But why? Why would he do that? Why would anyone . . . "

"Oh, I don't know. I'm not sure it's what he wants, per se. I just don't think he can resist. I don't think it's in him."

Heinrich thought a moment. "But then they'll leave, yes? Their aim is to leave the hotel? So all we have to do is stay right here."

Prince of Nightmares

"You can't stay here forever, Heinrich, plugging holes with the Bible and repeating your little prayer. They're not monsters from a fairy tale."

"Worked so far, hasn't it? Tell me it hasn't worked!"

"You're not listening to me. If they set foot beyond the Ballador, they will be the dominant race on the Earth. No one can fight them. No one can defeat them. They'll be gods. Gods who can extend life into eternity and thrive on pain. What do you think will become of the world?"

Heinrich's voice, when he eventually spoke, was very quiet. "An apocalypse."

"Worse than that, Heinrich. So much worse. It will be the very realisation of Hell."

"Oh God." He covered his face with his hands. Out in the hall there was a loud thud as an unfortunate soul was thrown from their room. "But what . . . I mean . . . What can we do?"

"Kill Victor."

Heinrich was silent a moment. "No. I don't think I could do that."

"Well, we can kill ourselves." Gia laughed. "I think we're still able to do that much. Beyond that I think we have maybe one chance. We have to run. We have to get out of here and go. We need to alert someone before the union can happen, but it has to be now. We can't wait."

"No, no," Heinrich said. "We can't. I tried. We won't make it."

"What do you mean you tried?"

"The woman. I mean . . . There was a woman. Outside. She forced me to come back."

"A woman made you come back?"

"I couldn't get past her! She had . . . some kind of power."

"What about your power, Heinrich? What about your will? You told us you could shape the dreams with your mind. Were you lying about that?"

"No, but . . . but that was different!"

"I don't think so. You should see it out there. Their world

is bleeding into ours and changing the laws of reality. Our world is becoming the nightmares, but you can control the nightmares, can't you? I don't think your grandmother's superstitions would do the slightest bit of good for anyone else. The only reason they're working is because you will them to. I think if you wanted—and you were brave enough— you could get us out of here."

"But the woman . . . "

"She can't stop both of us, Heinrich. Whatever she is."

She thought she could see him quivering in the darkness, a black shape shivering among black furnishings. He was shaking from fear. "You'll . . . you'll come with me?"

"It's our only chance."

He didn't say anything for what felt like a long, long time. At least, he didn't say anything to her, though she thought she could hear some sputtered words under his breath, like he was trying to talk some sense into himself. At long last she heard him sit upright and let loose a long, deep breath. "All right," he said. "I'm ready."

She found his body in the dark and moved in close behind him as he opened the door. There followed the unsettling sound of thin pieces of paper fluttering to the floor. He stepped out into the hallway. "Take my hand," he said, without looking back.

The corridor had morphed again, becoming a narrow funnel of molten metal. Heinrich raised an arm to shield his face from the heat and sparks as they danced through the shimmering air. The walls were lined with hundreds of red hooks and on each was skewered a cut of meat taken from a guest. They sizzled in the furnace. Heinrich blinked against the searing light of the white iron floor. "I can't," he said, gasping on cooked oxygen. "Can't . . . "

"You can," Gia said, closing the door behind them. "You need to focus."

He closed his eyes and the heat intensified, the walls around them glowing with supernatural incandescence. The meat burned and turned to cinder on the hooks, which in turn began to soften and melt. Bursting bubbles in the floor and wall let loose scalding steam and yellow flame.

"Heinrich?"

He opened his eyes wide. For a moment, Gia saw the man before her disappear inside a black thundercloud. Then the scene before her flashed out of existence, blown away like dust from a shelf. The light of scalding metal was snuffed out, plunging them both into darkness.

When Gia caught her breath, she found she was standing on carpet at the far end of what was probably a perfectly average hotel hallway. Her grip on Heinrich's hand tightened. "I can't see anything," she said.

"Shhh," he replied. The sounds of violence persisted from the rooms around them. It was clear all he'd done was forge them a path through the carnage.

Gia heard the snap of his lighter and saw a small white flame appear. It lit just a small portion of the way ahead.

"Come on," he said, and tugged at her arm. They marched together through cold shadows, glancing back and forth across the hallway as the lighter illuminated one door after another. Room 11, room 10, room 9, room 8. At the end of the hall Heinrich stopped. "Wait," he said. "Just . . . "

What happened next took Gia back to the theatre. The end of a convincing performance. The house lights come up. The performer sees her audience. They're on their feet. They applaud.

"No!" Heinrich cried as the Residents advanced. "Get back! Leave us alone! I deny you! I deny your existence. I deny you my fear! *Hier leg ich mich schlafen, keine Nachtmahr soll.*"

Gia put a hand on his shoulder. "Heinrich."

The floor ahead of him dropped out of existence, floorboards melting into the void as a large, round shadow rose up before them.

Heinrich squeezed his eyes shut. "I don't see you! I deny you! I don't see you!"

John McNee

"It doesn't matter," Gia told him, her tone sympathetic if not quite bordering on pity. "*I* see them."

"What?" He opened his eyes, turned and saw her, for the first time, as she truly was. A resurrected corpse. A purple-skinned assemblage of broken bones and congealed blood. He stared into her cold, red-veined eyes and wanted to weep. "Gia. No . . . "

Black vines wound their way around his arms and legs. Thorns pierced the skin. The lighter in his hand went clattering to the floor. He turned away from Gia and met a face he recognised like his own. Silver liquid poured down its lumpen, exaggerated features in a steadily bubbling stream. Its pink lips parted to reveal rows of black teeth glittering like daggers.

"Sorry," Gia said. "But they need everyone for what they've got planned."

29

"**You need me** to go willingly, don't you?" asked Victor. "That's what this is about. For you to get what you want, it has to be my choice."

"That's right, Victor," said Mr Ballador, rubbing his eyes. He looked exhausted. In the time they'd been talking he'd begun to visibly age, skin losing its colour, voice getting weaker, the flesh getting thinner on his bones. It appeared to Victor as though their conversation, along with his disguise, required more energy than he had in store.

Maybe, Victor thought, if he just kept him talking long enough . . . "You need me to join you voluntarily. You need me to trust you."

"That's right, Victor."

He nodded. "So tell me about Josie."

Ballador glowered at him. "That's a dead end . . . so to speak."

"What you said about her being born here, about assigning her a mission in the womb, that wasn't the half of it."

"It's complicated. Hard to explain."

"You appeared to Gia wearing my face, speaking with my voice. Before I even arrived. Why did you do that? How did you even know who I was?"

"I did say there would be holes, didn't I?"

"You were always able to reach Josie, weren't you? She had nightmares often enough. I remember them. That was you, wasn't it? Checking in, reminding her of your demands, learning everything you could about me."

Ballador sighed. "It isn't . . . it's not as precise as that."

"We were married for fourteen years," he said. "That's a good long time. She could have brought me here at any point she wished, but she didn't. She resisted for fourteen long years and, when she couldn't take any more, she finally did what you wanted. She booked the room and then . . . then . . . " He couldn't finish the sentence. He sank down onto the sofa.

"You'd love to be able to absolve yourself of all guilt, wouldn't you, Victor?" Ballador spoke calmly, with something that sounded a lot like sadness. "You'd like to be able to say I made her do this. That none of it was her own doing and *certainly* none of it was yours. But we both know that isn't really the case, don't we?"

"I just want the truth," said Victor.

Ballador frowned. "No you don't. But even if you did I couldn't give it to you. Maybe Josephine could. Maybe. But she's gone." He gripped both armrests and slowly raised himself onto his feet. "I'll tell you what I do know. This house makes flesh of thought. And if you really wanted to see your Josie as much as you claim, you'd have seen her by now."

Victor stared back at the figure now towering over him. He racked his mind for something to say, some riposte that would put Ballador on the defence and extend the discussion. He opened his mouth, but no words formed on his lips.

Ballador's smile was all triumph and sympathy. "Time to move on, eh Victor?"

That might have been enough to provoke a reply, but before Victor could speak, the door was thrown open and Gia was striding towards him, her steps making bloody footprints on the rug. She snatched his hand into her own and pulled him from his seat. "Come on," she said, dragging him into the bedroom.

He didn't resist. He trailed along behind her like a lost schoolboy until they reached the doorway, at which point she pushed him through ahead of her and cast a glance back to

Ballador, who flashed her a yellow-toothed grin, before she closed the door.

"Gia . . ." Victor stood in the middle of the floor, head bowed, wringing his hands. "I just . . . I want you to know . . ."

"Don't tell me you're sorry," she said as she came towards him. Her limbs creaked as she moved. "I don't give a shit how sorry you are. Just tell me you'll do what he asks."

Victor turned, forcing himself to look at her blood-flecked features and ragged razor-blade smile. "What are you talking about? No. No, didn't you see him in there? He's falling to pieces. If we just keep him waiting long enough—"

"What?" she interrupted. "You think we can just walk out the front door? Have you thought to take a look at yourself lately, Victor?"

He hesitated, and then walked to the other side of the room to the dressing table. The man who stared back at him from the mirror was his forty-year-old self. The skin on his face was tanned and tight. The bags, hoods, and wrinkles around his eyes had peeled back to nothing, exposing bright whites and pupils of vibrant blue. His hair had grown back into a brindled crew cut, covering his scalp. In short, he looked young again. He put his hands to his face to confirm the fact.

"You're not holding him back," Gia said, following him to the mirror. "Not so that it matters. It might look like he's falling apart, but every drop of energy he loses finds its way to you. It's been going on for days, probably from the moment you arrived. The longer you keep him talking, the longer it takes. But it doesn't stop anything."

Victor ran his fingers across his cheek, feeling its taught strength. "How? How do I stop it?"

He felt Gia shrug as she put her arms around him, pressing her broken body against his back. "Fight him, of course. But I don't think you really want to do that, do you? I think you want to join him."

"Like hell. You think I don't know my own mind?"

"You don't. Your grief's got you all confused, thinking you need to redeem yourself, prove yourself to be a good man. But the world isn't shaped by good men, Victor." She hooked a discoloured thumb towards the sitting room, where Mr Ballador patiently waited. "They knew exactly what they needed when they set their sights on you. They could have had Heinrich, with all his boastful powers and lust for depravity. But they recognised even a professional sadist doesn't have it where it counts. You're a different breed, Victor Teversham."

He didn't speak for a few moments. When he opened his mouth, his words were very quiet. "*If* I went through with it," he said. "Do you have any idea what that would mean?"

Her head nuzzled at his shoulder. "It means we could finally leave this place." Cracked lips brushed against his neck. "It means the start of a new life."

"For us, maybe."

"That's right," she said. "For *us*. Together." Her arms pulled him closer. "All I ever wanted was to lead an extraordinary life. By the time I came here my hopes for that were all but gone. Your life, too, was over. Think about that. This is a second chance to have everything we want."

He forced himself to turn away from his image and face her. His own handsome, youthful features made a startling contrast to hers. How things had changed. "I did this to you."

"No, Victor."

"Yes. Everything you've gone through. The pain you've suffered. It's all my fault. I unleashed it. But it's nothing compared to what I'll do . . . if I let him in."

She grinned, showing rows of shattered teeth through the tears in her cheeks. "Oh, Victor. Worth it!" She laughed. "All worth it."

In spite of himself, he smiled. "You really mean that, don't you?"

She cocked her head to one side, letting a strand of hair, thick with congealed blood, fall out of her eyes. "Whoever wants to be born must destroy a world," she replied, moving in for a kiss. "And honestly? I've never been too fond of this one."

Their lips met, his warm and wet, hers cold and leathery. Her tongue found his, tasting of salt and copper. He returned the kiss and saw her eyes close, but kept his eyes open. He put his arms around her, stepped to the right and turned with her, tilting her body so that he could see its reflection in the mirror.

He ran his hands across her gnarled, dead flesh, tasted her blood in his mouth and watched. His eyes travelled the length of her, from her diced ankles to the top of her blood-smeared head. He heard Ballador's voice—his own voice—in his head.

"See it. Change it."

When Gia finally broke the kiss it was with lips as full, warm, and soft as they'd ever been. She threw her head back, returning his gaze with clear eyes, sparkling with life. She grinned, making dimples in cheeks that were otherwise without blemish, in a face of ivory skin devoid of a single line. When her head turned sharply towards the mirror, the curls of hair that danced about her shoulders shone lustrous and clean.

"Oh Victor." She peeled away the bedsheet to stand naked before the glass. In every way remade. Re-imagined. Perfect.

She spun around and into his arms, knocking him onto the bed. He felt the air go out of his lungs, bursting from his mouth in an unexpected, albeit genuine, laugh. She lay on top of him. His body felt her warmth. His eyes saw her beauty.

"Where shall we go first?" she asked. She spoke breathlessly between kisses, fingers undoing his buttons. "When we leave?"

"I hadn't . . . hadn't given it much thought," he said, struggling to answer through his own laughter.

"Let's go to Paris," she said. "Can we?"

"I don't see why not," he answered, eager to be free of the burden of decisions, happy to let her make all their plans. "If that's what you want."

"We don't need to stay long," she said, pulling open his shirt, kissing his chest. "I have some friends there. I'd like to teach them something new."

E velyn couldn't bring herself to look at the hotel as they passed through the gate. She rested her elbow against the passenger side window and put her hand to the side of her head, blocking the view.

Harry swung the car about and parked at the bottom of the hill, from where a speedier retreat could be made. He turned to Evelyn. "You can stay here if you want. You don't need to come with me."

She stared into her hand and saw it was shaking. "I'm sorry. It's just . . . even after all these years—"

"You don't need to explain," Harry said. "Anyway, odds are everything's fine and I drove you all the way up here for nothing, so try not to worry."

"If it's not," she said, turning her head slowly to face him. "If the worst happens, just remember, they don't *belong* in this world. And they can't defeat a strong mind."

"Gotcha." He winked, stepped out of the car, slammed the door behind him, and stood there a moment hoping what he'd just said wouldn't be his final words.

He went around to the rear of the car and opened the boot. He took out the gun and a small torch, and then started up the slope to the hotel. The Ballador loomed over him, perched at the top of the hill like a horned demon, black against the deep purple sky. The sun hadn't yet risen above the mountains, but it was clear that dawn was well on its way.

When he reached the front entrance, Harry peered in through the windows, seeing nothing but darkness, then pushed open the door and stepped inside. The lobby was empty and unlit.

"Hello?" He dared not raise his voice above conversational volume.

There was no reply. Members of staff were supposed to be out front twenty-four hours a day. The most likely scenario was that they'd been called away to another part of the building or were simply neglecting their duties. He knew, instinctively, that wasn't the case. The place looked abandoned, but it didn't *feel* that way. There was a heavy atmosphere all around him, as though crowds of silent spectators clung to the shadows.

He crossed to the front desk, passing the lounge bar on the way and seeing it was just as dark, just as empty. All the tables were wiped clean, all the chairs neatly aligned. He stepped around to the other side of the desk and checked the office, but there was no one to be found. He did at least find some light switches and tried them, but they did nothing. The computer behind the desk was dead. The phone, too, when he tried it.

He was replacing the handset when he noticed the dark stain on the desk, difficult though it was to make out in the blue half-light filtering in through the windows. He took the torch from his jacket pocket, clicked it on, and turned its beam on the stain. The light revealed a russet handprint set in dried blood.

Well, all right, he thought. *That tears it.*

He returned to the office and searched through the keys until he found one for the Honeymoon Suite, then marched out and up the stairs to the first floor landing, ignoring the way the shadows clung to his skin and the oppressive silence amplified every sound he made.

He raised his fist to knock on the door, and then hesitated, thinking better of it. He tried the door and found it was already unlocked. "Victor?" he whispered, letting the door swing open on a room darker than the rest.

He held the torch in front of him, but its light seemed to dissolve in the shadows. "Victor," he barked again, only a fraction louder than before.

He waited, listening for a reply, but all he heard was the soft, whispered sound of rustling paper. Eyes straining through the darkness, right hand gripping the revolver, he took a deep breath and advanced.

Evelyn sat silently in the car for a few moments, cursing her cowardice. She listened to Harry's feet crunching through the gravel to reach the rear of the car and heard the pop as he opened the boot. She considered stepping out at that point. She wanted to tell him the pistol wouldn't do him a damn bit of good, but she knew he wouldn't listen. A moment later he moved off, towards the hotel, and she stole a glance out the window in time to catch sight of his dark shape as he strode up the hill.

When he was out of sight, she bowed her head and cursed the fear coursing through her veins. Returning to the Ballador, being back on the grounds felt like the last four and a half decades had never happened. Half-remembered fragments of the nightmares she'd suffered and long-since repressed came rushing back to her. The power, the pain, and the promises of worse to come.

She clenched her fists, squeezing until the nails dug into her skin, made her bleed, made her gasp. "Focus," she told herself, speaking aloud in the car. "Forget your fear."

She made the effort to breathe calmly, slowly, as though exhaling her own terror, then raised her head to stare out through the windscreen, fixing her gaze on the oak tree just fifty yards or so across the grounds.

A woman gazed back at her. Tall and slim, with short black hair and a long grey overcoat. She stood perfectly still, fixed in place like a mournful soldier at attention, her eyes locked on the infamous Evelyn Burgess.

Evelyn didn't jump, didn't scream or throw her hands up

over her face. Her fear was gone. She'd expelled it. What she did was sit patiently, as still and silent as the woman in front of her, and let the seconds accumulate between them.

When she was quite sure the woman was real, that she wasn't going anywhere, and that she wasn't a threat, Evelyn stepped out of the car and slowly closed the distance between them.

When they were close enough to speak, she smiled sadly. "You look just like your mother."

The early morning breeze whipped at Josephine's hair and coat. She peered back over her shoulder and stared up at the gradually lightening sky. "We don't have much time, you know."

"I was afraid of that," Evelyn admitted.

"You have to bear some of the responsibility for where we are now. We all do." Her words carved through the fog of Evelyn's mind like a blade.

"More my fault than anyone's. But, what can I do?"

Josephine turned back, facing her with sombre eyes. "Everyone inside now bears the stain. They can't be allowed to leave. Not one."

Evelyn nodded, recognising the truth when it was spoken. "What about you?"

"I can't go in there," said Josephine. "I have to keep my distance. But I'll be here. Until it's over."

They said no more to one another. Evelyn did an about turn and walked back to the car. She lifted the jerry can from the open boot and carried it up the hill, into the hotel, as focused, fearless, and determined as she'd ever been.

Harry stood in the bedroom of the Honeymoon Suite. The bed was empty, but light shone around the edges of the door to the en suite. He could hear the shower running within.

It felt like he stood there a long time, swaying on his feet, acutely aware of the surreal atmosphere. It drenched his skin.

When he did move it was with immediate, unexpected

potency. He ran across the room to the door and threw himself up against it, finding it locked. "Victor!" His fists pounded against the wood. "Victor, let me in! Victor!" He turned into it with his shoulder and tried to break it open. And again. On the third try the lock shattered, the door swung inwards, and he was engulfed in a billowing cloud of steam. He skidded on tiles slick with condensation, threw out his hand to steady himself, and caught the sink. Pulling himself towards it, the steam rolled back and he saw the bathroom mirror. The words, scrawled in lipstick: *God forgive me, I married an evil man.*

"Victor!" He staggered towards the bathtub, shower still hissing, hidden by its plastic curtain. Fearing the worst, he snatched it in his fist and hauled it back.

The Drowned Maid, tendrils twisting through the spray, turned her crater-black skull towards him and shrieked. He let loose a panicked cry of his own as he stumbled back, slipped and went down.

Her serpentine body erupted from the tub, hit the tiles, and came rushing towards him like a tidal wave of oil crashing on the shore. The tips of her innumerable tentacles drummed like the hammers of a typewriter on the ceramic. Harry kicked at them as he slid his way back towards the wall but without enough strength or speed to make a difference.

Her hands grabbed for his ankles, fingers like fused black needles digging into his skin. He kicked out, heels squeaking on the tiles and slapping his palms against the floor in a desperate attempt to find purchase. Her fetid body corkscrewed its way on top of him, grinding against his legs, pinning him to the floor. He could feel himself screaming but couldn't hear it over the sound of her grunting—loud and rhythmic as the coughs of a motorcycle engine.

Harry lashed out with his arms, fists bouncing against her jittering shoulders like they were rubber. Her neck strained and stretched, black ligaments popping to send her formless face rearing up into his, vomiting black spit, black teeth, and a black tongue from a black throat.

He screamed, caught like an insect in her trap. Screamed, spasmed, smacked his skull against the tiles and thought, *Oh, you stupid fuck. You imbecile.*

She can't defeat a strong mind.

He squeezed his eyes shut, telling himself he wasn't really there, that the bitch wasn't real, even as he felt her dress spreading out beneath him. It flowed like black mercury, coating the backs of his legs and bubbling up over his waist, forming an intimate cocoon of cold liquid, just enough to drown him.

He clenched his jaw tight, pretending he couldn't feel her slime-slick tongue as it lapped against his cheek. He listened past her hungry moans, focusing on the whispering scratch of dry wings, at once both immeasurably distant, yet unbearably close. He felt past the ghostly weight of her thickening tar embrace to sense the only true pressure on his body—the invisible form that had made a throne for itself on his chest.

With a considered, fluid motion that a moment before had felt beyond the realms of possibility, he raised his palm and slapped it down *hard*.

And somewhere far away the Drowned Maid screamed.

Opening his eyes felt like prying open a closed wound. Reality was another layer of torture, but he fought with it to force his eyelids apart and found himself on the Honeymoon Suite's bed, sprawled out on his back in the half-light, staring up at the ceiling. The cornicing grinned down at him. Turning his aching head to the right he saw the torch on the floor, still lit, a cone of white light shining on the pistol where he'd let it fall. He wondered at what point on entering the suite the visions had jumped him.

Sitting up, he looked down at his right arm, still lying across his chest from when he'd slapped himself. He lifted

Prince of Nightmares

his hand and saw the devastated remains of a huge black moth, wings and legs in fragmented pieces sticking to his palm and shirt front.

For a moment he thought he could hear the Drowned Maid slinking away through the shadows, injured, powerless and without anchor, seeking a hole to disappear into.

But, as he listened, he realised that what he really heard was music. Dusty old swing band stuff. It drifted through the wall, from the suite across the landing.

Shaking the fog of forced slumber from his mind, he rolled out of bed, gathered up what he'd dropped, and went in search of the jazz show.

E**velyn moved quickly.** She strode through the entrance, across the lobby and past the dining room to get to the rear part of the hotel. She never slowed her pace, knowing better than to linger in the silent rooms and hallways where even the air seemed unduly calm and calculating. She recognised the tranquillity for what it was—a façade, a cellophane disguise masking the scars of sin. It might be enough to trick an ignorant visitor, but Evelyn knew better. The insanity of a place beyond Ballador had crept through the building like a disease, poisoning every grain and fibre.

It was a sickness for which she could conceive only one cure.

She decided to start from the back and work her way forwards, taking it as a sign of good luck—rather than an omen of doom—when she entered the extension and discovered a black lighter on the floor. At the far end of the hall she found the floor littered with crumpled papers. She took the Bible pages for kindling. Then she opened the cap on the jerry can and started pouring.

She was relatively conservative about it, knowing a little could go a long way and not wanting to splash any on herself, but she tried to be quick, only moderately slowing her pace as she retraced her steps through the ground floor. She took a detour into the dining room, making sure a few of the tables got a good soaking, then continued into the bar and lounge. By the time she reached the lobby she still had a good half of the can left.

Prince of Nightmares

She put the cap back on and started up the stairs, passing the suites on the first floor and walking to the far end of the hall on the second. Again she opened the can and started walking backwards, dousing the floor, walls, and doors as she went.

She was out of breath on reaching the top of the stairs. She turned her head away from the fumes and caught the sound of music, drifting up from the floor below.

And, though she hadn't heard it in over forty years, she recognised it at once, "I'd Rather Be The Girl In Your Arms" performed by the Jean Goldkette Orchestra, 1926. It had been an old favourite of Fergus McLoughty's. He'd brought it to the Ballador in a box of records when the Peter Project moved in. Before he was paralysed, McLoughty had loved to dance and, under Evelyn's gaze, he was able to do so again. The Goldkette number saw frequent play through those months. Many of them had brought music to the house, she recalled. Almost all of it was left behind when they fled.

Evelyn gave the jerry can a little shake and found there was still about a quarter cup left. She poured it out over the stairs as she descended, following the echo of Frank Bessinger's tenor, then let it drop. She reached the landing as Harry emerged from the Honeymoon Suite. He looked sluggish, like he'd been smacked around the head.

"I smell gas," he said, squinting at Evelyn through his glasses. "What's with the music?"

Evelyn pushed open the door to the Library Suite. "Let's find out, shall we?"

What she found, on entering, was the library of Ballador House, almost exactly as she remembered it. All the hotel's expensive interior decorations had been scraped or burned away, revealing dusty floorboards, torn curtains and empty, cobwebbed bookshelves on every wall. The new furniture, too, was gone, replaced with the few simple items she and her companions had required for a session. The old Victrola stood in the corner, record still spinning, though the song had ended. In the middle of the floor were twelve chairs, arranged in a circle and turned out to face twelve tilted dressing mirrors. In each chair sat one of the hotel's guests or a member of staff—Gia, Dennis, Mrs Dempsey, and all the rest. Many were nude, though some were dressed in the clothes they'd been wearing when the Residents had captured them. Each of them sat perfectly still, backs straight, hands on their thighs, staring with blank faces into their own reflections.

Sitting alone, in the centre of the circle, wearing pressed pinstripe trousers and a white buttoned shirt, was the young Victor Teversham.

"Come on in," he said. "We're almost finished." He spoke without moving his head, without looking up at her. He was careful to hold himself like a model being studied by an art class.

Evelyn recognised the layout of the chairs and mirrors. She knew the significance of Victor's position in the ring. She'd sat in the same place herself, many years before.

"What the hell, Victor?" Harry cried as he came through the door and laid eyes on a man who looked younger and healthier than himself. "What the hell?"

"Hello, Harry," Victor said. "A day early, are you not?" He flicked a pinkie towards Evelyn. "Who's your friend?"

"Evelyn Burgess," she answered, walking around to the right of the circle. "You could say we've already met."

"Oh really?"

"This is my mess, for the most part. I've come to clean it up."

"I see." Victor almost smiled. "And how do you intend to do that?"

"I've got a few ideas," said Harry. He stood just within the doorway, switching his gaze from one ashen-faced guest to the next, trying to guess if any of them would try to block his path if he tried to get past them.

Evelyn looked as though she was doing the same as she

flanked the perimeter. In truth, she was staring past the guests facing her, past Victor and the guests on the other side of him to the mirrors. She wanted to see the reflections in the glass. The first, opposite a drooling young man in boxers and socks, revealed only himself, Victor, and the people around them. The second was merely another angle on the same scene. When she saw the third mirror, she stopped.

It stood opposite Dennis, now hastily reassembled into something reminiscent of his old self and stitched back into his uniform. His jaw, like the other man's, hung slack, his mind and soul burned out by torture to leave only what could be manipulated by the Residents. Evelyn's gaze lingered on the reflection of his face in the mirror. Behind him sat Victor. And behind *him* stood a hunched old man in a baggy three piece suit. More precisely, he looked like a corpse propped up with a silver-handled walking cane. His wrinkled flesh appeared discoloured, rotten, sliding off the bone. His white shirt was stained with the seeping fluids of decomposition. They oozed out the ends of his sleeves, dripping from his clawed fingers. His thin lips were pulled back in a rictus grin and, as he turned his head towards her, she saw the eyes were gone from his head. Red light burned in both sockets.

Though he'd disguised himself in the likeness of Victor Teversham, Evelyn recognised him instantly for what he truly was. She'd seen him in enough nightmares to know by now.

"I see you," he said.

"It's been a long time," she answered.

He gave the slightest arthritic shake of his head. "Only moments."

"Victor!" Harry clapped his hands. "Snap out of it! Come on. We need to go."

"All right," Victor said. "Just give me five minutes. Wait in the car, if you like."

"No, I don't think so," said Harry. "I think we need to leave right now." He took a step towards the circle and grabbed the nearest mirror, meaning to tip it out of his way.

In the glass, Evelyn saw Mr Ballador make a waving movement with his rancid hand. In the room, Victor made the same motion—as though a puppeteer's thread linked the two—and sent Harry stumbling back. He coughed like he'd been kicked in the chest and took another run. This time, Victor didn't bother with hand waving theatrics. His thoughts knocked Harry to the floor.

"Stay down, Harry," Evelyn warned, from the other side of the room. "You can't break the circle. They won't let you."

"I'm stronger than them," he coughed in reply, on his back and wheezing.

"No, you're not," she said. "Not this one."

In the mirror, Ballador grinned. Over his shoulder, Evelyn could see the reflection of another mirror and through that—reflection upon reflection—a slivered window into the world beyond. A place of impossible darkness and infinite hunger. His nest. His chrysalis. His birthplace. *Her* mind. A moment's glimpse was almost enough to seize her heart.

She spun away, pulse racing. Gasping, she squeezed her eyes shut and put a hand to her nose as the first droplets of blood began to fall. Behind her, Victor and Ballador chuckled in unison.

"What the fuck is going on," Harry asked, sitting up.

"Don't worry about it, Harry," said Victor. "It's fine."

"It's *not* fine," Harry yelled. "Christ, Victor, what's the matter with you?"

"Imprinting," Evelyn sputtered, between desperate breaths. She'd sunk almost to her knees, eyes still closed, heart still pounding. "Supplanting one consciousness with another. Like we used to do with insects. Only they're doing it to him."

"Not *supplanting*," Ballador rasped through a crumbling throat. "Joining." She knew he said it for Victor's benefit.

"That's all the nightmares ever were," Evelyn said, finding

it only slightly easier to speak. "Imprinting that didn't take. They needed the right subject."

Harry thought of the Drowned Maid and her moth. He thought of smashing it under his palm. "How do we stop it?"

"You don't stop it, Harry," Victor said, finally turning to look his friend in the eye. "Go wait in the car. I want this."

"You *what?*" Harry scrambled back onto his feet. "You *want* this? Why? 'Cause they gave you you're fucking hair back? It's a shitty deal, Vic! Don't be an idiot!"

"You don't know anything about it."

"I know more than you think. I've seen it with my own eyes." He pointed to Paul and Karen, both broken apart and put back together, minus a few intricate pieces, to sit quietly and emit brainwaves. "And what about these miserable fucks? You want to be a part of this? *This?* No. Not the Victor I know. They've gotten inside your head. Screwed you up somehow."

"We might have to hurt this one, Victor," Ballador said.

"He's a friend," said Victor.

"Even so."

"Maybe it's me," Harry continued, "but I'm struggling to see the appeal in bringing these things into the world to torture and kill and—"

"We haven't killed anyone," Victor said, parroting Ballador's words. "That's not how it works. They value life more than we do because they—*we*—need people. The world will destroy itself soon enough without our intervention. But we can *save* it, Harry! We can shape the world to whatever we want it to be and grant a little eternal life along the way."

Harry looked again across the row of wan, lifeless faces between them. Like cattle being milked by the synapses. "Eternal slavery," he said.

"For a few," Victor admitted. "But how many out there are slaves already? At least this way they can be part of the solution, each one a crucial cog in the machine, working for the betterment of humanity."

Evelyn could hear Ballador's voice overlapping Victor's now. The imprinting was nearly complete. Still shaking from the vision, she fought the urge to vomit and straightened up.

Harry's gaze had settled on Gia, sitting directly in front of him. Clothed in a thin white nightdress, grey eyes fixed on a distant point within the mirror's reflection, she looked undeniably beautiful, but just as brain-dead as the rest. "They're really important to you, huh?"

Evelyn opened her eyes and, for the briefest moment, in the periphery of her vision, caught sight of the Residents gathered all around her, talons out, teeth bared and mouths drooling in anticipation.

"Absolutely *crucial*," she heard Victor and Ballador say. "Every last one of them."

Evelyn knew what Harry was about to do before he spoke. She could sense his hand in his coat pocket, finger already on the trigger. With the Residents closing in about her, without the chance to give it much thought at all, she made up her mind to help him the only way she could. She pivoted on her heel and launched herself at the circle. "Harry!"

Victor/Ballador spun towards her, threw up his hands and sent her tumbling backwards through the air as, behind him, Harry drew the pistol and pointed it at Gia. "Let's see."

The gunshot roared in the same instant Evelyn collided with the bookcase behind her, though it was difficult for her to hear it over the sound of her own bones shattering. She plummeted to the floor, landing in an awkward jumble of withered limbs as Victor turned back towards Harry and, with a motion just as focussed, just as violent, sent him spinning back into the opposite wall. The pistol, snatched from his hand, clattered across the floor to land in a skidding halt within the safety of the circle.

Evelyn lifted her head and felt blood come pouring down her face in an urgent stream. She raised herself up on a broken arm to see Gia in a similar state, writhing on her back at Victor's feet with a smoking hole in her chest. "Victor," she gasped. "What . . . what . . . ?"

Victor, still seated, held his hand out in front of him like a claw, directed at Harry, pinning him to the wall. He glanced down at Gia, saw her wound and, with a thought, healed it.

The girl immediately ceased her frantic kicking and sat up, hands pressed to her breast, where the bullet had entered. "That fucking hurt," she moaned.

Victor ignored her. His attention was now entirely on Harry. "Dear oh dear, Harry," he said. "Deary deary me. Nice try, though."

All around her, Evelyn could feel confusion among the Residents, disruption in the ether. Shooting Gia had certainly rattled the psychic chain but hadn't been enough to break it.

Harry was stuck fast on the wall, as though an invisible railroad spike had been hammered through his sternum. The pressure was so great he could barely breathe. Frothing spittle flew from his lips with every desperate gasp.

Victor looked over his shoulder to where the gun had landed. He lingered on it, frowning. Evelyn could see him from where she lay. She saw his expression change, saw the thoughts behind his eyes. She kept watching his reflection in the nearest mirror as he turned back towards Harry, his newly young face suddenly lined with something approaching fear. "Where did you get the gun, Harry?"

There were tears on Harry's face. "Victor," he croaked, struggling to speak.

Evelyn saw the most terrible grin spread across Victor's face. "Hard to believe . . . it never occurred to me. But you've always been able to lay your hands on whatever was required. Getting whatever I needed. Whatever Josie asked for."

Harry knew where this was headed. "Victor," he said again. "Victor, I'm sorry."

"It was you." Victor's grin became a sneer. "She got it from you."

Harry's face was red. His body quivered. Words strained

to escape his throat through a wall of pain, fear, and remorse. "I . . . didn't know . . . what she'd do with it."

"Liar," Victor yelled and clenched his fists. Harry's eyes popped wide as his torso crumpled inwards, crushed like an old beer can. Blood erupted from his mouth in a vivid torrent.

In the mirror, Evelyn could see what remained of Mr Ballador—rags of a suit clinging to rags of putrescent flesh, all but faded away—shuffle forward to stand beside Victor and applaud.

His mouth empty of blood, Harry let out a terrible scream, ending the moment Victor's thoughts cut a crimson slash across his face.

"Yes," said Ballador, speaking with Victor's lips. They bent Harry's leg forward, snapping it at the knee. "That's it."

Evelyn, helpless and defeated, could feel her own pain pushing through the shock, crowding in at the edges, ready to push her off the ledge into unconsciousness. Letting her head fall, leaving the awful sight of Harry behind, her eyes came to rest on the revolver, just a few steps across the room, yet oh so far away.

She looked on as a wisp of black cloud, flickering with occasional lightning, spiralled down towards the pistol, wrapped itself around the handle and picked it up. She watched as the cloud rolled back to reveal the hand of a man dressed in a mud-spattered black and red check suit, hair pulled tightly across his head in a greasy comb-over, lips painted pink.

Heinrich hadn't moved from his position in the circle. By some fortune, the pistol had landed nearest him, the only member of Victor's congregation who had a shred enough of will to do anything with it. He gazed down at the weapon, turning it over in his hand, and then raised his mascara-lined eyes towards Evelyn.

With her own eyes she pleaded. With everything she had, she *begged* him.

And she watched, holding his gaze, as he put the barrel to his own head, gave a gentle smile, and pulled the trigger.

32

The gunshot brought the curtain down.

The bullet cleaved a hole through Heinrich's temple and exploded out the other side of his head in a lurid spray of blood, brain, and bone. But, in comparison to most, he got off lightly.

The psychic chain—the unseen framework that had made the whole ritual possible—shattered with the end of Heinrich's life. So too did the mirrors, every one blasting outwards, erasing the final image of Mr Ballador and showering the room with fragments of glass. Heinrich's head lolled backwards from the shot, and then pitched forward, pulling his body from the chair. The others followed him to the floor, tipping from their seats in perfect synchronicity. Gia, too, gave a little twitch of her head, as though the lights had just gone out, and lay back down as Victor, arms and legs suddenly gone slack, dropped hard onto his knees, then fell forward, hitting the floor with his face.

A fraction of a second later, Harry, without anyone to hold him up, did the same.

Evelyn shivered where she lay, her ears filled with the screams of the Residents. She was unable to block them out, as though her head was a balloon, inflated with the sounds of all their frustrations and fear. She squeezed her eyes shut, clamping a hand to her blood-slick brow, afraid it might finally pop, spraying her brains across the floorboards with Heinrich's.

At the last, desperate moment, the screams cut out. It

wasn't that they ended. She knew, somewhere, they would continue. But her link to them was severed.

In the library, all was silent.

It would be nice, she thought, to just let her head sink forward, lie down with the rest of them, and go to sleep. How much her wailing body would love for her to just give up. And yet, even as she thought it, her limbs were moving, foot pushing against the wall, forearm pressed to the floor, raising her up and awkwardly, painfully, dragging herself across to the other side of the room.

She didn't hold anything back, moving as quickly as she was physically able, weeping through her agony but refusing to yield. With her body in motion she was able to identify where the pain was coming from—fractured wrist, broken ankle, cracked ribs, and broken collarbone. She guessed she only managed to escape a broken hip because the ones she had were made of titanium. What good fortune that seemed now.

She crawled her way past the Ballador's guests and staff, each of them sprawled out in the circle they'd made. None moved, but Evelyn wasn't about to take that as an indication that she was out of danger. Heinrich's final act had shocked the Residents, wounded them and driven them back, but it was, at best, a temporary fix. Whether it took them minutes or hours, they would soon find a way to return.

Sweat and blood were running into her eyes and dripping from her chin by the time she reached Harry, finding him a pale-faced panting wreck in an even worse state than her. His shirt and jacket were soaked through with blood, lumps in the fabric showing the places where broken ribs had split the skin. The leg Victor had broken lay at an acute angle, almost wrenched free of the socket. Blood bubbled on his lips with every breath.

"Harry," she said. His hooded eyes were bleary and unfocused as they rolled round towards her. It was clear his injuries would kill him, likely in just a few moments. But perhaps, if she tried, she could keep him alive long enough for help to reach them. "Just hold on," she told him, blinking the tears from her eyes and focussing on his. "This might hurt a little."

It didn't happen all at once. Though she'd once helped a crippled man walk with the power of her mind, the circumstances had been altogether more favourable. She started with the cut on his face, holding the vision clear in her sight, letting reality bend to her will at its own leisurely pace. Nothing happened for just long enough that she began to fear that her gift had deserted her. But then the wound healed, forming a neat seam, one end to the next, like the closing of a zip-lock bag.

Next was his leg. It slid suddenly beneath him, twisting back into place with a dreadful *crunch*. A moment later, his chest made a similar sound, inflating to release the crushing pressure on his lungs, ribs slipping back beneath the skin and realigning, each one announcing its recovery with a wet *snap*.

Harry made what appeared to be an inverted scream, arching his back and sucking air down his throat in a long, desperate gasp. His eyes widened, finally focusing on Evelyn. "I'm sorry," he said, choking through blood and saliva.

"Don't be," she replied. "We're not done yet. Can you stand?"

He cringed at the thought, but nodded, then rolled onto his side. He moved stiffly, slowly, still in a tremendous amount of pain, but his muscles responded to his commands under Evelyn's gaze. He raised himself onto his knees, put his arms around her, and then stood, dragging her up along with him. Bent at the hip and on broken limbs they hobbled together towards the door, each one supporting the other as they stepped out onto the landing.

"Wait a moment," Evelyn whispered, fighting to speak through pained breaths. She went into her pockets and produced a ball of Bible pages and Heinrich's lighter. She put one to the other and threw the burning pages onto the stairs to the second floor.

The flames caught at once, blossoming blue and yellow, chasing the trail of petrol up onto the top floor and down the hall. It was an instant corridor of flame.

She repeated the trick once they'd limped their way down to the lobby, this time letting Harry pitch the ball into the lounge. It was cremated instantly in the flames that leaped from the floor, spreading back through the bar and beyond.

They held onto each other as they turned their backs to the fire and staggered across the lobby, through the door, into the dawn.

In the darkness, Victor heard a voice like his own.

"Get out," it said. "Get the fuck out!"

He opened his eyes to see black smoke, drifting across the ceiling. For a moment he was paralysed, unable even to recall *how* to move his limbs. Only gradually did his senses return to him, bringing with them the smell of smoke, the roar and crackle of the flames. His legs felt like they'd gone to sleep, but slowly, the more he willed it, the feeling returned. He flexed his fingers, finding them stiff and resistant, like his muscles had turned to rusting iron. It pained him to sit up, to crane his neck and look around. Gia lay beside him on the floor, unconscious but breathing.

He put his hand on her shoulder and shook her awake. "Gia," he said. "Gia, come on. Get up. We have to . . . we have to leave."

She moaned, but didn't open her eyes. "Can't," she whispered, placing a hand against her stomach. "I don't . . . feel well."

"Come on," he insisted, giving her another push. He looked across to the other side of the circle of bodies, where Heinrich lay, the pistol still in his fist.

Leaving Gia for the moment, Victor rolled onto his front and crawled across shattered mirror fragments to reach the weapon. He wrenched it out of Heinrich's dead hand and rolled again, over onto his back, still trying to kick some life into his legs.

Sitting up, he came level with Dennis. The waiter was awake. He'd managed to prop himself up against a chair, but now appeared out of ideas, content to sit where he was and let his head bob listlessly on his shoulders. He surveyed the room with an empty gaze, unable to process any of what he saw.

Victor knew there was no sense in trying to save him. And he wouldn't bother trying to save himself. He would sit and wait for the flames to consume his body. It might be more humane, Victor supposed, to put a bullet in his head right now.

The thought had barely formed in his mind when Dennis gave a woeful little cry . . . and exploded. Whatever threads had been holding him together for the ritual finally snapped. His torso burst beneath him, unleashing a deluge of blood and organs onto the floor. His head sank forward as his skin melted, face sliding from his skull to leave only grinning red bone. The silver earring remained in place over his eye, clinging to a stringy piece of cartilage.

It was more than Victor wanted to see. He threw himself forward onto his knees and started to crawl back to Gia, keeping his eyes fixed on her, ignoring the rest of the guests as they went the way of Dennis.

Karen bubbled away into slime beneath her pyjamas. Paul curled in on himself, his whole body fossilising, snapping into an ugly crystal contortion. Mrs Dempsey, with the saddest of sighs, unravelled again, her insides spilling out across the floor like the contents of an upturned picnic basket.

"Gia," Victor called again as he reached her, grabbing her pale, thin arm in his free hand and pulling her up. "Gia, please. Come on!" Fighting against the protestations of his aching body, Victor hauled them both to their feet.

"What's happening?" She coughed through the smoke, waving her hand in front of her face, barely managing to put one foot in front of the other.

"We're leaving," said Victor, leading her between the disintegrating bodies and out of the door, onto the landing.

A wall of orange flame flanked them on the left, raging hot enough to suck the oxygen from their lungs. Victor staggered right and almost tripped down the stairs, fumbling through the smoke for the wall, pistol still clutched in his hand and using his elbow to feel his way. Choking, stumbling, nearly half-blind, they made their way down. Gia's white nightdress was stained dark grey by the time they reached the bottom.

"Come on," Victor repeated, pulling her across the lobby.

"Wait," she said, when they were just a few steps from the door. "Victor, please wait."

"We can't," he said, spitting phlegm from the side of his mouth. "We have to—"

She halted. The change was so immediate, so assured, that Victor was thrown off balance. His hand slipped from her arm and he went down, hitting the floor on his side. Pain rattled his bones.

"Gia," he moaned, blinking away stars and looking up to see her standing tall, hands held out in front of her, ignorant of the smoke and flames all around, utterly lost in the contemplation of her fingers.

Her pale, perfect fingers. She watched as the colours changed, blotches of black and brown blood gathering under the skin. She saw the purple veins rise on her forearms and the skin peel back from her fingertips.

Victor tried to stand, fighting off the hangover fugue weighted on his limbs. "Gia, please." He held his hand out towards her, grasping through smoke. "Please, come on. We can fix it. *I* can fix it. You know I can! Gia, please. *Please!*"

When she raised her head, he saw her beautiful grey eyes were filled with blood. Dark red tears stained her ragged cheeks.

It was all over for her. She knew it even if he didn't.

She didn't say anything. All she offered him was a glance

and a disappointed sort of smile. Then she turned, and with the few steps she had left, strode into the flames.

Daylight.

Victor emerged from smoke and heat into the shock of fresh air, blinking soot-stained tears from his eyes to meet the morning. Behind him the flames intensified, chasing each other through the rooms and up the walls, shattering windows and spewing a tower of thick, black smoke into the sky. He limped down the path with faltering steps, wishing for his walking cane and struggling to see the way ahead through the tears.

He paused halfway down the hill, blinked again and rubbed the grit from his bloodshot eyes. When he pressed his thumb to his eye he saw Gia, the after-image of her last, regretful smile, seared into his vision. For a fleeting moment he imagined her dancing through the flame, making balançoires and pirouettes, even as her body burned. The fantasy brought no comfort.

He opened his eyes, squinting through the pain as the world before him came into focus. A fat line of grey became the path down the hill. A large dark blur at its end formed smooth curves and edges, revealing itself as the Bentley. Two more shapes—indistinct enough to pass for cloth sacks of waste, lay beside it in the gravel, propped up against the driver's side.

His grip tightened on the pistol and he started moving. He didn't need to see them. He knew exactly who they were.

"Harry," he growled, as he came within a few steps of them. His voice sounded like grinding rocks, his throat burned dry by the fire. He raised the pistol, pointing it at the blur on the right. "Harry," he repeated, raising his voice above the pain it caused him.

The blur on the left lifted her red and silver head. "You needn't bother. He's dead."

He stopped, keeping the gun trained where it was, watching the dark, crumpled shape in front of him. "What?"

"Only moments ago," Evelyn said, sounding almost as choked up as him. "I tried to save him. I mean . . . I did what I could. But illusions only last so long."

With his free hand Victor wiped again at his eyes, rubbing the last of the soot, tears, and stains from his sight. When he looked again, he found the gun was pointed at a dead man. Harry sat with his back against the car, legs splayed out in front of him, arms limp atop his thighs. Behind the tortoiseshell glasses his eyes were only half open, like his mouth, from which hung a long string of bloody spit. It quivered in the early morning breeze, the only part of him that moved.

Victor glanced up and caught his own reflection in the driver's side window. For the merest fraction of a second, he mistook the bald, bug-eyed pate for Mr Ballador, before recognising himself. Watery blue eyes peering out of sunken sockets. Sallow skin pulled too tight across his skull. A walking corpse in a white cotton shirt stained by smoke and blood. Good old Victor Teversham, unburdened of his youthful disguise and looking ancient and broken again.

The sight made him sick. He lowered his gaze back to Harry. He stared at the gun in his hand, and then very slowly turned it towards Evelyn.

She chuckled bitterly at the sight of it, laughing in spite of the pain it caused her. "Please . . . Please do." Her voice was coloured more by exhaustion than sadness, though there was a little of that too.

He held the gun on her for a few seconds, just in case he suddenly found the desire to shoot, then let his arm go limp, allowing the weight of the gun to pull his hand down to his side.

She gave a derisive little snort and rolled her eyes, then turned her head sharply away from him, looking out towards the loch.

He followed her gaze down to a point on the pebble shore, where a woman stood alone, facing them. A slender, dark figure, framed against the reflective glare of the water, she might only have been a mirage. Yet he knew she was more than that. He knew she waited for him.

"Go on then," Evelyn sighed, almost too bored to speak. "Go have your little moment."

Victor shuffled away from her as she nestled in closer to Harry's corpse, resting her weary head on his shoulder.

He dropped the gun somewhere between the car and the shore. Victor felt it slip from his fingers, but he didn't care and didn't look. His attention was on her. He kept her in his sights, afraid to blink, afraid to glance down even as he stumbled over patchy ground. All the theatrical vitality had dissipated from his body, returning the old pains, the old lethargy, the old, desperate yearning to just lie down and die.

His body cried out to him from the pain, from the age, the exhaustion and, deep within, something more. An icy void, squirming like a cancerous octopus, slowly taking form in his gut.

Lurching through the pebbles to reach her, his mind swam with awful questions about their life together, their love (if it ever had been that), her death and all the monstrous brutalities he'd seen and wrought in its wake. He had so much he needed to know, so much he needed to say, yet when he finally came to a halt and stood, swaying unsteadily before her, close enough to touch, all he could say, in a bleak, guttural croak, was a single word.

"Why?"

She took a long time to answer, first glancing over his shoulder to the burning hotel, then returning her gaze to him.

No emotions lined her face, but in her eyes there appeared to be the smallest measure of sympathy. "I'm sorry," she said at last. "It's just . . . how it had to be."

The sound of her voice brought fresh tears to his eyes. He felt an ache at the back of his throat as he tried to suppress a sob, even as his emotions overwhelmed him. It stung to imagine how pathetic he looked—a withered old fool, eyes narrowed with tears, bottom lip quivering like a child's. "Am I an evil man?" he asked.

Her features softened at that. "Oh, Victor." She took a step towards him, raising her arms.

He backed away, shaking his head. "Am I?" Having found the courage to ask, he demanded an answer. "Am I an evil man?"

"No," she replied, with unspeakable sorrow. "Just an empty one."

She put her arms about him and held him close as he wept. The touch of her sent a shiver through his body. Her hair brushed his tear-stained cheek. Her scent filled his nostrils. She was real. Whether angel, ghost, or dream, it didn't matter. They were together again and for a fleeting moment, all that he'd done, all that he'd suffered, seemed worth it just to hold her.

"Shhh," she said, rocking him like a baby. "It's all right now. Everything's all right."

He felt a chill from deep within. "It's not," he admitted. "He's inside me."

She didn't release him, but there was an immediate, subtle shift in the way she held him. "You're certain?"

He nodded. "It worked. I don't think he knows it yet. It's like he's lost and confused, and doesn't know where he is. But he'll figure it out. And, when he does—"

"You know what he'll do."

"Yes." His grip on her tightened. "We don't have much time."

She pulled back, lifting his head from her breast, cradling it in her hands. "You want to stop him?"

John McNee

A dozen blood-stained faces flashed in his mind. Gia, Heinrich, Dennis . . . Harry. "I don't want to hurt anyone else."

Her fingers caressed his cheek, wiping away the tears. "I can make it so he never gets the chance."

"Yes," said Victor.

She had one hand on either side of his head. Fingers against his temples. "You won't ever see me again."

He nodded. "Just do it."

She smiled. It was a wonderful thing to see. "Goodbye, Victor."

Her thumbs plunged into his eyes and gouged them out of his head.

He screamed as pain exploded through his skull, plunging him into black. He threw out his hands towards her, touching nothing but air, and staggered forward, arms flailing, feet scattering pebbles, falling through space she had occupied less than a second before. He collapsed onto one knee, feeling it sink into the pebbles and the rush of cold water as it washed onto the shore.

Lost in darkness, he let his hands trace the destruction of his face, touching the blood as it spurted down his cheeks. His shaking fingers felt the wet, empty holes where his eyes had been. "Josie," he muttered, and then screamed. "Josie!"

She didn't answer, couldn't answer, because she was already gone. Now and forever. Yet Victor could hear another voice. Another scream of agony and anger, a cry so inconsequential it should have been easily eclipsed by his own, yet cut through his senses, sounding only in his ears, his head.

It was the scream of Mr Ballador. Trapped, neutered, inconsolable, he raged, howling through the prison walls of Victor's soul. Devoid of sight, he was powerless. Without eyes, the two of them were locked together, utterly helpless, united and alone, from here unto death.

Victor collapsed onto his back, sinking into the pebbles,

letting the water soak his clothes. This, he knew, was what she'd hoped for. Her endgame. Her answer. She'd found the Prince of Nightmares' perfect host and, at last, turned him into his jailer.

Victor felt a grin spreading across his face, even as the villain within him shrieked, voice rising in pitch and volume all at once. Soon it would fill Victor's head. It would be all he would ever hear. His master's voice. His *true* voice.

It sounded like Evelyn Burgess.

For the moment, other sounds of the morning remained audible, filtering through the prisoner's cries. Sprawled out on the shore, nothing to do and nowhere to go, Victor tilted his eyeless head towards the sun and let its soft light warm his face. He focused in on the sounds beyond Ballador. The quiet lapping of the waves. Birds in the trees. The furious tumult of the flames. And, somewhere beyond all that, still a long way off, the wail of emergency sirens.

He hoped they took their time.

About the Author

John McNee is the author of numerous strange and disturbing horror stories published in various anthologies. He is also the creator of Grudgehaven and the author of *Grudge Punk*, a collection of short stories detailing the lives and deaths of its gruesome inhabitants. *Prince of Nightmares* is his first horror novel.

He lives in the west of Scotland, where he is employed as a magazine editor.

Made in the USA
Monee, IL
06 February 2023

27229914R00125